HUNTING
DANGER

REDEMPTION HARBOR SERIES

Katie Reus

Cover art: Jaycee of Sweet 'N Spicy Designs
Editors: Kelli Collins & Julia Ganis
Author website: http://www.katiereus.com

Hunting Danger/Katie Reus. -- 1st ed.
KR Press, LLC

ISBN-13: 9781635560435
ISBN-10: 1635560438

eISBN: 9781635560428

Die with memories, not dreams.

CHAPTER ONE

—Family isn't always blood.—

Ice flooded Nova's veins as she reread the text from her best friend, Layla.

Check out my ring! Isn't it unbelievably fantastic? We need to get together and celebrate my engagement asap. Maybe we can do a spa day and get mud masks, the whole works. I know how much you love stuff like that. The text ended with some cute emojis.

But Nova knew something was wrong. The two words "unbelievably fantastic" were code words they'd developed when they'd been in foster care together. They'd had a foster parent who'd used the phrase all the time, to the point where it was beyond obnoxious. At least that foster mom had been annoying but harmless. But that was when their code phrase to indicate that something was wrong had been born. Not to mention Nova hated getting mud masks or anything to do with body wraps and "stuff like that." Something Layla knew.

This whole text was wrong. Layla was in trouble.

The ring itself was gorgeous, but now Nova wondered what the hell was going on.

She texted back immediately. *I love the ring! You're right, it's unbelievably fantastic! I've saved up time off, let's plan something immediately! Girls' weekend!* Then she added some silly emojis of her own.

Her friend texted back less than two minutes later with details on a spa close to where Layla lived. It was in Montana, far away from South Carolina, where Nova was, but it wouldn't be a long plane ride. The name of the spa was vaguely familiar too so it was likely plush.

She texted back. *I can get a flight for tomorrow and meet you there. Do you need me to set anything up?* Her heart raced as she sent the text off.

Perfect. And don't worry about a thing, I'll make sure we get the VIP treatment. Call you soon. XOXO

Nova sent back hugs and kisses to her friend then set her phone down for all of a second before she jumped up. Changing out of her pajamas, she quickly tugged on jeans and a long-sleeved sweater then pulled her hair up into a ponytail. It was close to midnight, so no one should be at the office. Obviously Layla didn't feel safe telling her what was wrong, but something was. Nova had to find out what was going on.

As she headed out, she scrolled through her phone and called Brooks, one of the cofounders of Redemption Harbor Consulting, where she worked. He owned a private jet and the company used it fairly frequently. She'd never asked for any sort of favor like this and felt strange doing so, since it was pretty huge. Jet fuel was expensive. But she also didn't care. She would do anything for her best friend. The girl who was more a sister to her than her actual blood-related sister was.

And that was a whole other can of worms she wasn't even going to think about right now.

Brooks answered on the first ring. "Hey, Nova. Everything okay?"

It was definitely too late for her to be calling, and it wasn't like they were friends. Sure, they were friendly, and Nova was most definitely friends with his wife, Darcy. But it was strange that she was calling him. So she wasn't going to waste time bullshitting him.

"Look, I have a pretty big favor to ask, and I feel weird asking, but I need to borrow your plane. Would it be possible for your pilot to file a flight plan and take me where I need to go?" She could easily just get a plane ticket, but she wanted to get there as soon as possible and not deal with bullshit TSA or airports, in case she and Layla needed to make a quick getaway. She wanted to be with her friend, like *yesterday*.

There was a long pause, and she thought maybe she'd overstepped her bounds. Then he said, "Of course. He'll take you wherever you need to go. This about a job?"

She paused, trying to gather her thoughts. "No. This is personal. And I really appreciate your discretion." She wasn't exactly asking him not to say anything to anyone at the company, but she was implying it. Even if it was stupid, because right after this she had to call Skye and tell her that she was taking time off for the foreseeable future. She wasn't coming back to South Carolina until she was sure Layla was all right.

"You know the whole team has your back if you need something." Brooks's words were neutral enough, but he was clearly fishing for information. Not that she blamed him.

She was asking to borrow his plane, something that felt a little insane even though he could afford it. "Of course, I do know that. Like I said, this is just personal stuff, and I really appreciate you letting me use the plane." The billionaire cowboy was generous and kind and she'd seen the way he was with his wife. He'd screwed up once with Darcy, but since he'd won her back, he practically worshiped the ground the woman walked on. Nova liked the guy for that alone. "I can text you all the details or just get in contact with the pilot myself." She had Jim's info because Nova was the executive assistant/operations manager of Redemption Harbor Consulting, and they'd used the jet for on- and off-the-books jobs.

"Just text me. I'll set it all up. And...call any of us if you need anything."

"I will, thanks." Once they disconnected, Nova set her security system as she stepped out of her house. Before she headed to Montana, she was going to do some research on her best friend's fiancé.

Layla had told her only a little bit about her boyfriend, who she was now apparently engaged to, and Nova had never thought to look the guy up. Her friend had seemed happy and said she loved where she was living. Nova had been so busy with her new job and settling into Redemption Harbor that she'd taken everything her friend had said at face value. Because why wouldn't she? They'd never lied to each other or hidden anything.

But something was clearly wrong. And if Layla was in a bad situation, Nova was going to get her out. She had a few tricks up her sleeve, after all. The only thing she could think of was that Layla was being abused or something was wrong with the man she was engaged to. So she probably needed an escape plan. Getting out of a spa should be easy enough.

Yeah, Nova knew she was jumping to conclusions, but she'd worked for the CIA once upon a time. She often went worst-case scenario in her head. It was better to be prepared than to be dead.

So right after she checked out the fiancé, she needed to pull up the schematics of the spa—which meant she had to go to the office. And she knew exactly whose computer she was going to use.

Gage "too sexy for his own good" Yates was a hacker extraordinaire who had all sorts of interesting programs on his many, *many* computers. Occasionally he let her "play on them," as he called it. She was familiar enough with some of the programs, even if she had no idea how they actually worked.

Once she had all the information she could find, she'd figure things out. Because if her best friend was being abused or needed help for any reason under the sun, Nova was going to get her the hell out of Montana.

* * *

Gage ripped off one of his boxing gloves and answered his phone before the second ring finished. "Hey, what's up?" It was way too late for Brooks to be calling. "We got a new job or something?"

"Maybe," his friend said, his tone neutral. "Got a call from Nova. She wants to borrow the jet."

He blinked as he ripped off his other boxing glove and dropped it to the bench against the wall alongside its partner. He hadn't been able to sleep so he'd decided to get in a workout. It was the only thing that seemed to combat his insomnia lately. He'd tire himself out until he was so exhausted he *had* to sleep. Because his waking thoughts were consumed with Nova Blaire, the woman he couldn't have. Shouldn't want at all. "Did she say why?"

"No. I didn't ask. She simply said it was personal. And then Skye group-texted us that Nova would be out for a few days, maybe longer."

Shit. He'd missed the damn text. "Seriously?" he snarled as he stalked from his home gym. "You didn't press her for more details?"

"Nope. Because she's a grown-ass woman and I'm not her keeper."

Gage cursed under his breath even as he started stripping off his sweaty shorts. He needed to take a quick shower, and then he was either going to call Nova or drive over to see her. Because asking to use the jet at the last minute? For something personal? No. That had bad news written all over it. And to hell with it, he was going to help her. Whether she wanted it or not. "Thanks for the heads-up."

"You also might want to know that I got an alert to my email that her security code was just entered into our security pad at work."

Gage cursed again. "Text me the flight plan info and tell the pilot not to leave without me." He hung up without waiting for a response. Then he checked his email and saw that, yep, he'd received an alert too. He just hadn't heard the email ping or the damn text over the sound of his fists beating against the punching bag.

After taking the world's quickest shower, he dressed and was out the door. His protective feelings for Nova were irrational but he didn't really care. Ever since he'd met the smart-ass woman, he'd fallen for her. And each day a little harder.

Who was he kidding? He was gone for her. But he was sort of her boss, and there was way too much of an imbalance of power between them. He would never cross the line or make her feel uncomfortable. But that didn't mean he was going to let her go headfirst into something without backup.

For all he knew, she didn't need backup and this was about some guy. But even the thought of that seemed off. And deep down, he didn't think that was what this was. Nova had a big heart, and if he was a betting man, he'd bet she was helping someone. Why she wouldn't just ask the crew to help her made no sense to him, considering that was literally what they all did for a living.

Redemption Harbor Consulting wasn't technically a consulting company. They helped people get out of bad or dangerous situations. Those who couldn't afford it, or, because of whatever reason, couldn't go to the authorities with their problems. Like in the case of Olivia, who'd been blackmailed by a former "coworker" she'd run jobs with. Jobs that involved stealing expensive shit. She'd had no one to turn to except her college friend Skye. So maybe that's what this was—maybe some gray-area problem Nova was dealing with.

He shook his head as he raced down the road. He was just flat-out going to ask her what was going on. There was no sense in trying to guess.

Even as he glanced at the clock on his dash, his heart rate kicked up a few notches because he knew he was going to see Nova in less than ten minutes.

Nova—walking, talking sex. With long, dark hair she usually kept twisted into some bun thing at the nape of her neck, sultry, pouty lips he'd had too many fantasies about, and long, long legs he wanted wrapped around his waist or draped over his shoulders as he ate her out. She was a wet dream. More than just the physical aspects, she was clever and a smart-ass, something he adored about her.

He had to stop thinking about her. That would do no one any good, least of all himself.

He had to get his game face on right the hell now. He had to put on that familiar mask of neutrality, pretend he didn't want to back her up against the nearest wall and kiss her until her knees gave out, every time he saw her.

Because he never wanted her to guess how badly he'd fallen for her. How badly he wanted to call her his own. No way would she ever be into him—she was a goddess, and he was, well, he knew who he was and he owned it. They were friends and colleagues, and he wouldn't screw it up and make it awkward by letting her know how he felt.

CHAPTER TWO

—Survive now, cry later.—

Nova frowned at one of the computer screens as she scanned the information she'd just unearthed. It was difficult to know if she was headed in the right direction, but Layla's fiancé, Brody Kingston, might have a couple shell corporations loosely attached to him. But she wasn't skilled enough to know for sure.

Which just pissed her off. She'd have to dig deeper. Unfortunately, that would take time. And she'd just heard a soft *beep beep* from one of the front doors, letting her know that someone was here. Considering the building's security, it had to be one of her own people.

She quickly sent a few files of info to her email to review later, then shut down all the programs she'd been using, grabbed her purse and stood. When she reached the door, she nearly ran into a hard wall of muscle.

Gage Yates.

Dammit. Why did it have to be him? The man who starred in all her fantasies? Of which she had far too many. And why the hell was he here after midnight? He couldn't be checking on her, could he?

She pasted on a casual smile even though her heart was racing out of control. For multiple reasons. "I see I'm not the only one working late."

His bluish-gray eyes narrowed ever so slightly as he looked down at her. Considering her height, it was impressive that he was taller. But at six feet three inches, Gage was taller than a lot of people. And the smartest, sexiest man she knew. That brain of his was ridiculous. She always felt a bit out of her league when around him. Which didn't help her sanity any.

"What are you doing in my office?" he demanded.

His tone made her straighten. Instead of answering, she decided to go on the defensive. Even though she'd only been an analyst with the CIA, she'd learned a lot of tricks during her training. "You said I could use your office anytime I wanted. Has that changed?" Her tone was butter smooth, over-polite. Which she knew would annoy him.

"No."

"Good." She slid past him, unable to avoid contact as her breasts brushed against his side. She really hated that even this little touch affected her so much. Especially since it made her feel like a pervert. Damn him, he should have moved.

As soon as their bodies touched, he jumped back as if she'd burned him. Seriously, the man was hell on her ego. They were friends, yeah, and he'd made it crystal clear that was all he wanted from her. Gritting her teeth, she started down the hallway but he stopped her.

"Nova. What's going on? Brooks said you needed the jet for something."

She glanced over her shoulder and shrugged as if it wasn't a big deal. "Just some personal stuff I need to iron out. Nothing big." Her voice sounded light enough and she thought she sounded believable. Now if she could get out of here before he continued questioning her, she should be good.

"How long are you going to be gone?"

She lifted her shoulder again as she took another few steps away from him. She needed to be gone now. Layla was depending on her. In addition to the shell corporations, she'd found a few images of Kingston with some men connected to a Mexican cartel. Not exactly a smoking gun, but…it wasn't good. "Few days, maybe. Not sure. Trust me, this is not a big deal. I just didn't feel like dealing with commercial travel and we have that sweet jet available for use." She laughed lightly, staying in casual mode. She had to keep her game face on right now.

He simply nodded, but there was an unfamiliar gleam in his mesmerizing eyes. "Call me if you need anything."

She headed out, glad to be away from him so she could breathe again. As soon as she got in the car, she shot off a text to Layla, even though it was late. *So excited to see you! Think I can get an early flight. When should I meet you at the spa?*

This time it took a few minutes for Layla to respond, and Nova cringed. Maybe she should have waited until morning? But no. Layla was two hours behind her anyway.

I've got two rooms booked for us right across the hall from each other for Saturday morning. Both under my name but if you get there early, just check in.

Sounds good. I'll probably show up early, maybe Friday, and get some extra pampering! Nova went heavy with the emojis.

Layla texted back more emojis, then, *I'm unbelievably excited to see you!*

Yep. Something was definitely wrong. And Layla was making it clear by using the "unbelievably excited" text again. Still, she texted back. *Me too!*

Nova didn't have many people in her life—other than the new circle of friends she'd started to create in the last year—that she considered family. Yeah, she fit in anywhere and had no problem being social. It was a learned skill she'd developed at a young age. But it wasn't the same thing as having a core group of people she trusted and loved. The Redemption Harbor crew was the closest thing she had to family. Other than Layla. And Layla... She couldn't lose her.

As she pulled out of the parking lot, she glanced in the rearview mirror. It didn't appear as if Gage was following her—and the thought was pretty silly—but she was feeling paranoid. Maybe she should ask the crew to help with this...

Nope. As soon as the thought crossed her mind, she shelved it. With the exception of Gage, who was currently acting as remote backup to the whole crew, everyone was off on different jobs.

She could handle this herself. And if she discovered that she couldn't, she'd call for backup then. No need to pull anyone away from other important stuff if this turned out to be nothing.

Though deep down, she didn't think this was nothing. Layla was a levelheaded woman. She taught high school math—though she'd decided to take this year off, and now Nova was wondering why. Dammit, she should have pushed her friend more about that. But the last couple times they'd talked, Layla had sounded rushed so they'd taken to simply texting lately.

As she headed home to pack, Nova received a text from Brooks that the pilot was now on standby. Perfect. That meant she could leave tonight. No way was she waiting until morning. Not after what she'd discovered about Layla's fiancé. At least she'd have time to dissect more information on the plane, and then maybe she'd be able to get a clearer picture of who he really was.

On the surface, he appeared to be a legitimate businessman, but he had some interesting ties to some very bad people. And if those ties went even deeper…that couldn't be good.

* * *

Layla forced a smile as her fiancé, Brody, stepped into their opulent bedroom. She'd lied and told him she had stomach cramps the last two days so she wasn't in the mood for sex. But she knew that excuse would only last so long.

His mouth pulled into the slightest frown as he noticed her cell phone in her hand. She was sitting back against the headboard, with pillows propped up behind her. He loosened his tie before stripping off his jacket. Tall with dark hair, dark eyes and a strong jaw, he was classically handsome. His teeth were damn near perfect and brilliantly white, and when he smiled, once upon a time, she'd felt so special that his smiles were reserved for her. Now…she had to fight off shudders when they were alone. "It's late to be on the phone."

The fact that he was mentioning it bothered her. When they'd first gotten together, she'd been blind to his faults because the man was so charming. Lately, however, she'd noticed that he could be controlling. It was frustrating, especially since she didn't question him about who *he* talked to on the phone or how late.

Turned out she should have questioned a lot of things a long time ago.

She shrugged and set the phone on the nightstand next to her glass of red wine and e-reader. "I just texted Nova. We're going to do a long spa weekend to celebrate our engagement." She nearly choked on the last word, but kept her perfect smile in place. Being around him now, knowing exactly the type of man he was, had her on edge, but she couldn't afford to show it.

She was a survivor. She'd grown up in the foster system and had learned from a very young age how to mask her emotions. Right now, it was saving her life.

The frown eased slightly as he continued to undress, heading for their walk-in closet. "When are you planning on leaving?"

She'd wanted to schedule something immediately, as in tomorrow, but had worried that would somehow seem suspicious. "I called the spa and our check-in date is Saturday." Even a few weeks ago, she would have asked him if that was okay with his schedule. And she cursed herself for it. But she'd fallen into a routine with him, as if she'd been seeking his approval. Looking back, she realized she had been. She hadn't lost herself completely, but she had let him take over certain aspects of her life. It had been easy enough, and almost a relief in a way, especially since she'd been taking care of herself for what felt like forever.

Brody stepped out of the closet wearing just boxer shorts. God, she hoped he didn't push the issue of sex. She would do whatever it took to survive, but it didn't mean she wanted to.

"I've got a thing this weekend."

She laughed lightly. "You always have a thing. Besides, this is a girls-only trip. You are not invited." Her tone was teasing.

And the charming smile he gave her, the one that had fooled her for so long, easily slid into place as he crawled onto the bed beside her. A slither of fear trickled down her spine, as it so often had the last couple days. She kept wondering if he knew what she'd seen. Surely he would have said something—or done something to her—if he had.

"You know how much I worry about you," he murmured, brushing his lips over hers. "I need you to take security with you."

She knew better than to argue. Not now. She'd balked a few times in the past at his demands, but now she had to play things right. Her life depended on it.

"You're always so protective." She mock pouted even as she shuddered inside.

"I protect what's mine."

She didn't think it was protect so much as control. "Fine," she said, as if she had a choice. "Two guys. And they'd better blend in."

His lips pulled into a thin line. "Three guys. Two beautiful women alone at a spa?"

She snorted, the reaction real this time. "Yeah, we're going to be surrounded by a bunch of *other* women. You're ridiculous. But I love it," she tacked on, even as she hated saying the words.

He kissed her again, deepening it, until she gently pushed against his chest. "Still have cramps," she murmured apologetically.

His jaw tightened in frustration, but he moved off her. "I need to get some work done anyway."

She just bet he did. "I'll probably read for a little bit then go to sleep."

As soon as he was gone from the room, she allowed herself a tiny modicum of relief. But not much. She didn't think there were cameras in their bedroom, but she was going to act as if there were. As if she was always being watched.

She needed to go to the authorities with what she'd seen. With what she knew. But she didn't trust anybody around here. The man she'd seen Brody kill had been a DEA agent. She only knew that from a news report she'd seen afterward. And one of the other men who'd been with him had been an agent as well. He'd done nothing as Brody had pulled out his gun and shot that other agent right between the eyes.

So now she had to get the hell out of here and find someone who could help her. Right now, Nova was literally the only person on the planet she trusted. And her best friend had once worked for the CIA. She would know exactly what to do. She was smart and resourceful and Layla was certain that her friend had recognized the code they'd used so many years ago.

An hour later, she was glad she'd taken extra precautions when texting Nova. Because Brody had done exactly as she'd thought he would. He'd come into their room when he thought she was sleeping and checked her texts.

She'd caught him doing it once before, and he'd been so unapologetic about it, as if it was the most normal thing in the world. He'd handed her his own phone then, telling her she could check his whenever she wanted. It had made her feel silly and stupid. Now she recognized his actions for what they were. He was checking up on her because he wanted to control her. And she wondered how long it had been going on. Probably since they'd gotten together.

She continued to feign sleep—something she'd also learned as a kid—and kept her body relaxed even as he slid into bed next to her.

Only a couple days to go, she told herself. Only a couple days and then she'd be free.

CHAPTER THREE

—I'm not weird. I'm a limited edition.—

Nova smiled at Jim the pilot as she reached the short set of stairs to the Learjet. "Thank you for getting here so quickly," she said, even though she knew it had absolutely nothing to do with her.

No, the guy was on standby because Brooks Alexander paid him a crapload of money. It was his job. But there was no reason she couldn't be polite.

He nodded once, his gaze sweeping over her appreciatively, but thankfully not in a creepy way, before he straightened. "Glad you're here. I've already filed the flight plan and done the preflight checks so we're ready to go as soon as you settle in."

She quickly moved up the stairs and froze the moment she ducked inside the plane—when she saw Gage sitting in one of the plush leather seats, a laptop in front of him.

"What the hell are you doing here?" Immediately she winced at her loud tone.

"I think I should be asking *you* who the hell *this* is?" He turned his laptop around on the small table as she stomped inside. She was vaguely aware of the pilot ducking inside then closing the hatch. But she ignored him as he headed to the cockpit, focused only on Gage.

She wasn't exactly surprised to see Brody Kingston's face on the screen. Damn it, she should have done a better job of erasing her tracks. Or maybe Gage shouldn't have been such a sneak. "You checked up on what I was doing?"

"Yep." There wasn't one ounce of apology on his face either. His annoyingly handsome face. That she wanted to punch just a little right now.

"Why?"

He snorted. "Don't change the subject."

She glanced over her shoulder as the engines rumbled to life. Then she turned back to Gage. "You need to get off this plane. You're *not* invited."

He stood, though he had to bend down slightly to avoid hitting his head on the roof as he towered over her. "I'm going. Now start talking."

Glaring at him, she took a seat across the aisle instead of sitting in front of him or next to him. Then she crossed her legs away from him as she strapped in.

"You can give me the silent treatment all you want," he said, dropping back into his seat. "I can just guess what you're doing. Did you date this guy?" He seemed to struggle with the question.

Frowning, she looked at him. "Seriously? That's the best you could come up with? No, I didn't date him. I don't know him. My best friend is engaged to him. And something is wrong." She sighed, realizing it was better to simply tell Gage everything she knew, which wasn't a whole lot. So she quickly ran through the texts she'd received from Layla.

In the background, the pilot let them know they would be taking off soon and to make sure they were strapped in. Both she and Gage ignored him.

Once she was done, Gage seemed somewhat more at ease. "That is definitely strange. Why didn't you just come to one of us? We would have come with you. Obviously." Now that frown was back and even deeper than before. He looked all sexy when he got frustrated like that, deep in thought.

Something she didn't care about. *She didn't.*

Nova looked away from him, trying to get her thoughts together. She wasn't used to asking for help. If something needed to get done, she did it. End of story. She'd learned early on that she was responsible for herself and couldn't rely on anyone else. It was how she'd survived.

Finally she turned back to him. "Everybody is busy on a job. Really important jobs. And you're their backup. I wasn't sure—and I'm still not sure—what's going on with Layla. Obviously it's not good, but I'm highly capable." Something she apparently needed to remind Gage of. She took Krav Maga, spoke multiple languages and had trained with the CIA. She'd been an analyst and not a field agent, sure, but she'd still had training. "If her fiancé is abusing her, I'll be able to get her out of a spa. I do have training."

"No one ever said you didn't."

She rolled her eyes. "You didn't even want to let me go on that little recon thing to an elementary school. You acted like I was completely incapable," she said, referring to an earlier job. Whenever she thought about how rigid he'd been, she got pissed. So she tried not to think about it.

"That has nothing to do with it."

"Then why were you so stupid back then?"

"Are you back to name-calling?"

"Apparently so, but you've moved on from jerkface and now you're elevated to dumbass." For some reason, Gage brought out far too many emotions in her. Emotions she was used to keeping locked down tight. It was beyond frustrating.

To her surprise, he snorted out a laugh. "I love it when you call me names," he muttered, and she believed him. "Look, backup is never a bad thing. You are part of this team. Maybe I *was* kind of a dumbass before, but we're all here for you."

She lifted a shoulder as the plane launched into the air. She didn't love flying. She didn't hate it either, but it certainly wasn't her favorite thing to do. Talking to Gage helped ease the tension inside her as she worried about her friend. "I know that. I just didn't want to drag anyone into this until I knew what was going on."

"Well, I did some more digging on the guy, and—"

"When?" The man had arrived here before her. "And how did you beat me here—are you planning on traveling with no clothes or anything?"

The grin he gave her was a tiny bit wicked, and though she doubted he intended it, she felt that smile all the way to her toes. Gah, why did he have to be so sexy? "I've always got a go bag—and I've been working on digging up information on him since I got on the plane. I saw your search, and you uncovered some good stuff, but it's just the surface. He's on the radar of the DEA. They suspect him of having something to do with one of their agents going missing."

Her eyes widened. "How do you know that?" Because it couldn't be common knowledge, and she wasn't sure that kind of info would be available for him to hack. But who knew.

"I called in a favor to a friend of mine, a guy I used to serve with. He told me off the record. Because the DEA doesn't have enough for a warrant to do anything to this guy. He's like Teflon. They suspect him of gun and drug running and more than a few unsolved murders. Maybe not him personally, but the guys who work for him at least."

"Oh God…" Nova swallowed hard. And Layla was engaged to this guy?

"Tell me about your friend. How she met him, anything you think might be important."

It went against her nature to open up so much, but she had to do it. "Look, if I tell you about Layla, I have to tell you about myself. And what we talk about stays between us." She looked him in the eyes as she said it. It wasn't like she'd had the worst childhood in the world, and she wasn't even embarrassed, not exactly. But that didn't mean she liked to talk about her past. Especially not with the man who starred in all of her fantasies. They were friends, sure. He was the one she'd called on New Year's when she'd needed a last-minute ride, and she joined him on stakeouts occasionally—and they often had early breakfasts together. But a lot of the time, she kept things very surface level.

"Everything we talk about stays between us," he said quietly. "Unless it's necessary to this job, I won't share anything. And even then I would ask you first."

She nodded once, believing him. He was a superb hacker and she knew for a fact that he hadn't dug deeper into her, and he easily could have. She'd flat-out asked him if he'd hacked into her past and he'd said no—and she believed him. He seemed to respect the privacy of his friends.

"I got put in foster care when I was fourteen. I wasn't in it for very long, not technically speaking. My mom had some issues. Drugs mostly, though it really comes down to self-esteem issues. So my sister and I got put in a home that already had another girl. Layla. We became tight. She's the sister I always wanted," she added, feeling only a little bit guilty. Her real sister wasn't a bad person or anything, but they weren't close.

Gage simply nodded and it took her a moment to continue. God, what was wrong with her? If this had been anyone else with the company, she wouldn't have an issue even if she didn't like talking about her past. But with Gage it felt more intimate somehow. Probably because she was attracted to him. Okay, definitely because of that.

"Anyway, we became really close. And when my mom got her act together, for the most part anyway, my sister and I went back to live with her. I was about fifteen then. Layla spent most of her time at our house after that. It's not that the foster home we were in was bad at all. Our foster mom was kind of annoying, but we all got incredibly lucky. And I'm still in touch with Mrs. Baker." The woman had actually been interviewed as part of her background check when she'd been hired by the government. "I know the foster system gets a bad rap—rightfully so in many cases—but she's one of the good ones. That's not really important to know."

"You can tell me anything and everything, whether it's related to this thing or not." Something about Gage's intense stare, the way he was focused solely on her, as if she was the only thing that mattered, unnerved her.

Nova glanced away for a moment as she cleared her throat. "We grew up together as sisters, and I'll give my mom credit; she never had an issue with Layla staying over so much. Probably because it kept me out of her hair. My mom had my sister on the beauty pageant circuit so there was no time for anything else other than that. She was convinced my sister would be Miss America one day." Nova shook her head, surprised by all the emotions that welled up as she thought about her family.

"Anyway, Layla went to school for education and I went to school for business. We roomed together, even waited tables at the same places throughout college. There is no one on the planet who I'm closer to. In the last year and a half, I've been so busy with work and she's been incredibly busy with her new boyfriend. Well, now fiancé, apparently. Every time we talked or texted, she seemed happy. There's no way she's involved with anything this Kingston guy is involved with. That much I can tell you."

"I believe you," Gage said quietly.

Even if he didn't, she was glad he'd said it. "The text from her, coming out of the blue like this, it scares me. And now combined with what I found, and with what you told me about her fiancé, I'm worried maybe that's the reason she's scared. Because I honestly can't see Layla putting up with abuse. But...that kind of thing just sneaks up on you." She knew that, not from personal experience herself but from watching her mom fall into the same trap over and over with abusive men. They'd be nice and charming at first, then convince her mom that she deserved what they doled out. Once her mom got clean, however, at least she'd found a good man.

Gage frowned at that. "I'll run all her information, her financials, anything I can. I'm going to invade her privacy."

"I figured you would have to." Nova might not like it, but she understood the necessity. "I pulled the schematics for the spa we're meeting at. If she needs to escape, I've already looked at different exits and I've been thinking about various escape routes. I haven't had time to come up with anything solid, and without talking to her in person it's impossible to know who will be with her or what kind of threat she's facing. But I'm trying to be proactive. There are a lot of ways two women could sneak out of a spa. Easily."

Gage looked slightly impressed. "It goes without saying that I'll hack into their security, and if she does need to escape him, and I'm thinking she does no matter what, we can work as a team to get her out."

Nova was silent for a long moment. "Thank you for coming with me." She hadn't thought she wanted backup but it made her feel more secure that Gage was with her. For more than one reason.

"So I'm not a dumbass anymore?"

She snorted slightly as she stretched her legs out. "I wouldn't go that far."

His lips kicked up, and once again she felt the effect of it straight to her core. This man was going to kill her with his raw sexuality. Since they had a couple hours to go, she slipped off her shoes and pulled out her own laptop. "Can you send me what you've got so far? I want to read up on this douchebag."

"I've already sent you a bunch of files."

She smiled softly at him, not surprised at his efficiency. "Thank you."

He sort of grunted and turned back to his own laptop.

She tried not to stare at him, at the way his jaw ticced slightly as he focused on whatever he was reading. But it was hard not to admire his strong profile. He was built like a runner, even if he was into martial arts. He had that whole long, lean, muscular thing going on, and she very much liked it. She liked everything about him. He'd recently gotten a haircut so his dark hair was cropped close to his head. She wished he'd left it longer, but for selfish reasons. She loved the way it used to fall over his forehead so that he'd get frustrated and shove it back—and flex those ridiculous arm muscles.

At that thought, she turned away, or she'd end up staring at him and getting nothing done.

* * *

Gage glanced over at Nova as she intently read something on her computer. They'd been at cruising altitude for a while and it was smooth flying. Not that he cared about that. No, it was hard to focus on anything when he was only a few feet from Nova.

And they were alone.

God, the woman was incredible. He still couldn't believe she'd thought she could go off on her own for something like this without anyone to back her up. He knew she was capable, but the thought of her not having any backup pissed him off. And okay, it scared him. He wasn't used to being scared.

But she was this bright, wild star that had come into his life, and the fact that he was even thinking in such stupid terms told him how far he'd fallen. But she was. And the thought of anything happening to her... Nope.

"Did you get scholarships for college?" he asked, even though it had nothing to do with what they were dealing with. He'd never dug into her past because he hadn't wanted to cross that boundary. Not with her. Never with her.

She blinked and looked at him almost as if she'd forgotten he was next to her. "Wha...ah, yes," she said, shaking her head slightly. "I didn't want to have a ton of loans—ha, who does—so I went to a community college the first two years, then transferred to a bigger university. Luckily I was able to get a lot of scholarships. Finding them was tough, but Layla and I both did what we had to do. And we worked our asses off. I swear I never slept during college. I was either working or studying. I don't think I could have gotten through those years without her. She was my rock."

In that moment, Gage decided he'd do whatever it took to save Nova's friend. He understood having friends like that. Friends who had your back no matter what. And it was clear that it would rip her apart if anything happened to Layla.

He just hoped Layla wasn't somehow involved in whatever her fiancé was involved in. He hoped she was simply looking for a way to escape the man. So far he hadn't been able to find any financial links between the two of them, which was good. But in his experience, people could fool you. Still, Nova was a good judge of character. He was going to trust her friend simply because Nova did.

CHAPTER FOUR

—Things can always get worse.—

Nova jerked awake as the plane suddenly dipped. "What the hell is happening?" she asked, even though she knew Gage couldn't possibly have any idea either. He looked as if he'd just woken up himself, his laptop closed next to him. It flew forward as the plane dipped again.

The aircraft started to shake as it descended at a much-too-rapid pace. Her stomach jumped into her throat as Gage shoved up from his seat.

"Sit tight and stay strapped in!" He hurried up the aisle, bracing himself against the seats as he made his way to the cockpit. When he disappeared inside, she heard him curse.

The overhead lights flickered on and off and when she looked out the window, all she saw were stars and moonlit pasture—and mountains in the distance. She gripped the seat as she tried to process what was happening. Was this turbulence or…something worse?

A moment later the plane started to even out, though it was still bumpy. And they were still descending too fast.

Way. Too. Fast.

"What's going on?" she shouted.

"Pilot is dead," came Gage's sharp reply.

Holy shit! Ignoring his earlier order, she unstrapped and hurried to the front. If they were going to make a hard landing, she figured it was better if they were close together—that way, Gage could attempt to do a back-heavy landing with the plane. Oh my God, if that was even possible. What the hell did she know about planes? Maybe they should rush to the back instead?

As she reached the cockpit, she winced as she stepped over the pilot's slumped-over body. Gage had pushed the guy out of the chair and taken over the pilot seat.

She jumped into the copilot seat and strapped in, her stomach in knots. "What can I do?"

"I can't get anybody on the radio." He cursed again. "And some of these functions aren't working. We're losing fuel much too quickly."

Her heart rate increased even more. She knew exactly zero about planes and flying. Need a translator for Russian? She was your girl. Need some Krav Maga lessons? Again, she was your girl. Had a question about what type of dress you should wear to a formal wedding? Yep, she was your girl. This? Nooooo.

She hated feeling useless but shoved the panic back down. She wasn't going to freak out right now. She would save the crazy for later. If she survived. "Please tell me you have experience in flying planes?" It seemed too much to hope.

"I've taken some classes. And I've done some simulations. That's it." He didn't spare her a glance as he flipped a couple switches.

Nothing seemed to happen though. They were still descending pretty fast. Too fast, it felt like. "So what's the plan?" Because they definitely needed a plan.

"I'm going to try to land. As long as we have enough fuel and these functions remain working, we should be able to." He motioned to one of the screens but it meant nothing to her. She might as well be looking at Portuguese.

Then he muttered, "Landing gear isn't working."

What. The. Hell.

The panic she'd been trying to bury skyrocketed again, this time wrapping around her throat with icy fingers, but she simply nodded as if she understood exactly what he was saying.

She stared at him as he attempted to fly while he tried to get someone on the radio. It was pretty clear no one was responding, if his curses were any indication. God, if he hadn't come with her, she would have been alone right now as they crashed to the ground.

She'd be dead. The coldness was back, sweeping her under.

Don't panic. No, do *not* panic. Leaning forward, she placed her head between her legs and took a few deep breaths trying to get herself under control.

The last thing Gage needed was to have a freaked-out woman on his hands when he was trying to save their lives. Still, how the hell could this be happening? Their plane was going down? Jim was dead? And she didn't even know where they were. They'd been traveling for a few hours so she knew they had to be somewhat close to their destination, but God, what if they couldn't land? What if they crashed? Well, she certainly wasn't going to ask Gage.

The ground was coming up so fast beneath them. She stared in horror as their plane dove down, down, faster and faster, terror gripping her throat so tight she couldn't make a sound.

Time didn't seem to exist as Gage shouted, "Brace!"

Still strapped in, she held on for dear life, all her muscles pulled taut as Gage suddenly pulled up on the controls.

The nose of the plane lifted up as its belly slammed into the earth. She jolted forward, her knee slamming into something hard in front of her as she was pinned against the harness.

"Hold on." Gage's words were tight as they flew across…a field.

She couldn't focus on anything around her, her vision going blurry, but she kept clutching onto the armrests. She was vaguely aware of pain in her left leg, but it was as if it was happening to someone else. The engine screamed, the noise deafening as they slid over the ground, faster, faster.

"Nova!"

She blinked at Gage's sharp tone and looked at him. What…

They weren't moving anymore.

"Are we stopped?" she whispered, shaking all over. She looked out the window to see pastureland illuminated under the moon and stars.

"We're okay." Suddenly, he unstrapped and was kneeling next to her in between their seats.

Without thinking, she grabbed his shirt and tugged him to her, planting her lips on his for one brief second. He was stiff, clearly surprised, but she didn't care. She then wrapped her arms around him, pulling him into a tight bear hug. His embrace was just as hard.

Then it was over. He pulled back and scanned her from head to toe.

"Oh my God! We're alive! Right?" Her heart was racing so fast, she swore it could jump out of her chest.

"Yeah, we're okay," he rasped out. "Are you hurt anywhere?"

"No." The answer was automatic, but even as she said it, she didn't think it was true. She tried to catch her breath. "Well, my knee hurts. And…I'm sore everywhere."

"You're going to be sore for a while," he murmured, gently lifting the leg of her jeans. When he pushed it up, he winced slightly. "It's swelling, and will probably get worse."

"That's okay. We're alive," she whispered again, unable to believe what had just happened. "Oh, God, Jim."

She turned to look at their pilot, but Gage cupped her cheek gently.

"Yeah, I know. We're going to make sure he's taken care of properly. But I need you to come with me. I want to get you out of the plane while I grab our bags and other things. Can you walk?" he asked, standing.

"Yeah." Or she hoped she could. She winced as she stood, but nothing was broken. She was almost positive. Either that or she was so hopped up on adrenaline she couldn't feel it. Her hands were shaking, and with every breath she dragged in she felt as if she'd come apart at the seams.

"We got this."

She simply nodded as she leaned on him and stepped into the body of the plane with him.

There was so much they needed to do. Mainly, find help. Her phone…

Was in her bag in the back. Damn it. And her laptop had been on the seat next to her. They'd be able to make a call as soon as they got out of here though. Or maybe Gage would do that once he got everything.

A shudder snaked through her as more cold seeped into her veins. This time it wasn't from shock or anything else, but from the temperature. An icy wind whistled through a giant hole near the back.

Seeing that, seeing the destruction in front of her… She swallowed hard, forcing the bile back down. They were alive. She had to remind herself of that.

* * *

Gage stepped out of the battered but mostly whole plane, jumping down onto the disturbed grass and dirt. Immediately he sought out Nova. He'd managed to get her out of the plane about ten minutes ago and had moved her far enough away from it that she wasn't at risk if there was an explosion. He wasn't sure what the hell had happened, but the transponder had been removed. And there was no way it was a coincidence that something had happened to the pilot *and* the mechanical systems.

They hadn't failed completely but that shit wasn't normal, especially not the fuel leakage. Not with a state-of-the-art Learjet 75. But that was something he would have to worry about later. Right now, the only thing he cared about was getting Nova away from here and contacting someone for help. Unfortunately, neither he nor Nova had service on their phones, he couldn't find the satellite phone, and both their laptops had been battered to hell. He was fairly certain he could retrieve the data on his later, but for now it wasn't working. So they needed to get somewhere else and try to get service.

He slid his backpack on and picked up hers as he stalked toward her.

She'd been so shocky in the plane, and he thought she might still be in a little bit of distress. She'd held up well, but as they'd crashed, she'd looked as if she had completely zoned out. As if she wasn't seeing anything at all.

He'd had to call her name half a dozen times once he'd brought the plane to a stop, just to get her attention. Then she'd seemed to somewhat snap out of it.

At least they didn't have any broken bones. Her knee was busted up and it was going to be hell for her to walk. But he'd be with her every step of the way.

He'd been in worse situations, at least. Maybe not actually crashing a plane, but he'd been shot at and had been stuck behind enemy lines for a couple months. Twice. He knew how to survive.

And he had no doubt that Nova could, too, because the woman was a survivor. They would get through this. Then they'd get to her friend—and he'd figure out what the hell was going on.

Thankfully his watch was still in one piece, so he had the coordinates of the plane crash noted. And before they'd crashed, he'd seen a building. It could've been a house, a barn or anything, he wasn't sure, but he knew the general direction. So that was where they were going to head. Because they were in rural Montana. According to the coordinates, they were maybe nine hours from Billings—by vehicle. Which was their final destination. So they just needed to get to a damn phone. Then get a car.

Nova tried to push up as he reached her but he crouched down. "Stay seated," he said as he stretched her injured leg out slightly, being gentle with her calf. "How are you feeling?"

"Sore. But I feel a lot clearer-headed. I don't think I freaked out much...did I?"

"No. You didn't freak out at all." But she had scared him with her quietness. "I saw a ranch or house before we crashed. Due west of here, so that's where were going to head. You're in no shape to go far, however. At least not tonight. But I want to get a little ways from the crash site and build a fire." For a multitude of reasons. He didn't think it would explode, but on the off chance that something sparked an explosion, he was going to play it safe. It was cold, but not freezing. And he was armed, so if any wild animals came sniffing around they'd be okay.

Not to mention, he was partially worried there was some sort of tracking device on the plane. It seemed unlikely, but someone had wanted them to crash, so it stood to reason that whoever that was might track the plane and finish the job if they failed. Though...he couldn't imagine why anyone would want to kill him and Nova, specifically. Maybe him, but this trip had been last minute.

No, it was more likely that this had been a general targeting type of thing toward Brooks or his father. He shelved those thoughts for now. Not important.

"I'm going to wrap your knee tight and then I'll help you walk."

"I'll just slow you down." Her breath curled in front of her, soft white wisps of air.

"I'm not leaving you." He pulled out the small first aid kit he'd snagged.

"I don't want you to. I'm not a martyr. I'm just saying that if you want to go on ahead of me, I'll be fine. There's enough food and water in the plane for me to be okay until you get back."

He didn't care. He still wasn't leaving her alone. So he ignored her and instead said, "Tell me if this is too tight. We're going to need pressure on it, but not so much that you're losing circulation."

"Okay. Are you just ignoring what I said?"

"Pretty much." He worked quickly as he wrapped her leg, hating that they only had a basic first aid kit. Hell, he hated that they'd been in a plane crash. Seriously, what the hell? He wasn't going to allow himself to dwell on it. Not right now anyway. He was good at compartmentalizing, always had been.

"I really don't think I can go far tonight," she said softly.

"I know. We'll get a few hours of sleep and then head out in the morning. You think you could make it maybe half a mile or so?"

She nodded once.

He hated everything about the situation. But he stood and held out a hand to her. It was clear she wasn't going to be able to carry her backpack, so he quickly took his off and pulled out any essentials she might need and tucked them into his own.

"I can carry a backpack," she said when she realized what he was doing.

"Nah. It will just slow us down. Trust me. And in the Marine Corps, I had to carry packs with seventy or a hundred pounds or more. This is nothing."

"I can't tell if you're lying or not." She closed her eyes and rubbed her temple. "Normally I can tell."

"One day, you'll confess what my tell is." She'd once told him that he gave it away when he lied but he couldn't figure out what he did. And she was the only one who'd ever called him out on it. Worse, she was never wrong. He just hoped she never figured out how he felt about her.

Hoisting the backpack on, he wrapped his arm around her, and let her put her weight on him as they started walking.

"So…this should be filed as things that are *not* important right now, but I'm sorry I kissed you back there."

Hell. He hadn't been expecting that. Her sweet vanilla-and-cookies scent wrapped around him as tightly as her hand grasped his waist. "No worries."

"I was in shock. That's the only reason I did it."

The moonlight lit their way, highlighting a broad, open field that led up to a fence. From this distance, he couldn't tell if it was maintained or not. If it was maintained, that was a good thing. "You're great for my ego." He should have just accepted the apology and let it go. But it did sting that shock might be the only reason she'd kissed him. Which, like she said, was something that wasn't remotely important right now. Still.

She snorted. "I'm just saying…I didn't plan to do that."

"It's all good. We're good."

"Good," she muttered.

All right, then... How was that for awkward? She was silent as they slowly trekked across the field. He stayed aware, scanning their surroundings as they moved, and his weapon was tucked into a secure holster on his pants. But he could withdraw it in seconds. Even with her holding on to him.

As they finally reached the fence, he frowned. One of the bottom boards on the middle section was rotted through, but for the most part, the fence was standing strong. A standard wooden split rail for cattle. Hopefully there was human life nearby.

"I feel bad leaving Jim behind," Nova said into the quiet as he jumped over the fence.

"Me too." It went against everything inside Gage. Even if he hadn't known the man well, the concept of leaving anyone behind scraped at his insides. "We'll make sure he's transported back to Redemption Harbor. He'll have a proper burial." He helped her to maneuver over the fence, then felt like a jackass for enjoying the way she held on to him for a long moment to gather her bearings. She was in pain—he shouldn't like her holding him because of that. God, he was an asshole.

Her expression was pinched. "Look...I don't think I can make it much farther. I'm just tired. And you're the one carrying a big pack so I feel like a baby saying this—"

"We won't go much farther. And you're not a baby. We were just in a plane crash. A. Plane. Crash. Repeat that to yourself if you start calling yourself names again."

To his surprise, she let out a snort-giggle. "I feel like today can't get much worse. Hell, this *year* can't get any worse after what we survived, right?"

Oh, things could always get worse. But he didn't say that. He simply tightened his grip on Nova and kept going. As soon as they found a safe enough place, he'd set up something for them. It wasn't going to be comfortable, but he'd keep her warm. And more importantly, safe.

CHAPTER FIVE

—I'm going to need more coffee.—

"I'm impressed with your fire-making skills. And I'm being completely serious." Nova scooted closer to the small fire Gage had started. The man was remarkable. "If I had been by myself, I would have likely been killed by the elements. Actually, I would've died back in the—" Damn it. She did *not* need to go there right now. Her throat tightened as the words died on her tongue.

Suddenly, Gage was right next to her, wrapping his arm around her shoulders. She didn't even question it. She simply leaned into him and buried her face against his chest.

"I feel guilty that we survived." And it was crashing in on her as she and Gage sat in front of a warm fire. Alive and mostly okay. Sure, she was banged up and her knee throbbed, but they were still alive. And Jim wasn't. She realized she had no idea if he had a family. Not that it mattered. It was terrible that he'd died, regardless of whether he had a family or not. But she hated that she didn't know more about him. He'd been flying them across the country in the middle of the night because of *her*, and she'd only known his name.

Gage murmured something she couldn't make out as he rubbed a strong hand up and down her back. Seriously, if he hadn't been with her, she had no idea what she would have done even if she *had* survived the crash.

"I'm wiped," she murmured, letting the exhaustion sweep over her. She was tired of fighting it. She was afraid to go to sleep mainly because she was terrified of wild animals attacking them in the middle of the night. She was a city girl through and through. What the hell did she know about rural Montana? A bear might attack them while they slept. "What happens if a bear attacks us?" she whispered, pulling back to look at him.

Thankfully he didn't laugh at her. "I'll take care of it."

She believed him. Believed *in* him. "Okay."

He watched her for a long moment, as if he might say more, but then seemed to contain himself. "Come on," he said, even as he pulled a rolled-up poncho out of his backpack. "You can use the backpack as a pillow." He set it next to the poncho, so she did as he said and laid her head on it.

She was surprised when he curled up behind her, wrapping his arm tight around her waist as he pulled her close. Whatever cologne he had on was intoxicating—something she shouldn't notice right now. Or, not ever. His forearm was hard, the muscles pulled tight, but she held on to it as if it was a lifeline. She wanted to think he was holding her close because he had feelings for her, but she knew the truth.

Of course they would need to huddle close to maintain warmth. They'd both layered up with clothes and were sleeping close enough to the fire, but not too close, and body heat would help. At least the weather wasn't bitterly cold—and wouldn't be for another month or so—but she would be grateful when the sun rose.

Finally, Nova felt safe enough to close her eyes. Gage was behind her, holding her, his presence the only thing keeping her sane right now. And okay, she really, really liked the feel of his hard, muscular body pressed up against hers. It was almost enough to make her forget the pain in her knee. Almost. She'd thought about being held by Gage enough times that it was embarrassing, but never in these circumstances. She could safely say a plane crash had never been in her fantasies.

God, she hoped they were able to make contact with someone tomorrow. At least she wasn't supposed to meet Layla until Saturday, so as far as her friend knew, she was fine. Nova hoped that held true, that they were able to get out of here and contact the crew back home. Well, they weren't actually home, they were off on jobs, but one of them would be able to help.

"Someone had to have sabotaged the plane, right?" she murmured instead of going to sleep. Her knee hurt too much and she couldn't get comfortable.

Gage hadn't said much to her and she wondered if he was holding back on details.

There was a moment's pause and his grip tightened ever so slightly. "I wasn't going to say anything until later, but yes. It was sabotaged. The transponder was missing and there was too much engine failure. And Jim… He was dead when I got to the cockpit. There's no way some of the plane's electrical systems failed at the same time he died. I don't believe in coincidence."

"He could have had a heart attack."

"Maybe."

She didn't believe that either. Yeah, Jim could have, but the guy had been in his forties and appeared to be in excellent shape.

Nova snuggled closer to him, digesting everything he'd just told her. She was glad he was honest, even if the news added another layer of worry. She couldn't imagine someone targeting her specifically. That was crazy. But someone in their group was being targeted; likely Brooks or his dad. Or maybe this was about Redemption Harbor Consulting. They'd been involved in taking down some unsavory people. Most of those people were dead, however. And they were very careful about how they operated. No media attention, a fake social media presence, and a bunch of other precautions she didn't really want to think about now.

Why? Because there wasn't a single thing she could do about it if someone had targeted them. Not now anyway. She needed to start thinking in small steps. Like step one, get out of the wilderness alive. She barely remembered the crash or anything directly after. Everything was so hazy. A blur of loud noises and flashing lights. She must have been in shock.

As they lay there under a blanket of stars, Nova became very aware of something hard pushing against her butt. Even though she was exhausted, the feel of Gage's erection surprised her just a little bit. Okay, more than a little bit.

She stiffened slightly.

Gage cleared his throat. "I'm sorry."

"You don't have anything to be sorry for." She was just going to leave it at that. It felt weird to admit that she didn't mind his reaction to her at all, but she also did *not* want to talk about it. Not now. She knew guys could have weird reactions to adrenaline-filled situations. Maybe that's what this was. Or maybe he was attracted to her. Or…

She sure as hell wasn't going to ask him. Maybe later. When they hadn't just survived a plane crash. And when her knee wasn't aching and sleep was closing in on her like a tsunami.

Instead, she shut her eyes and decided to let sleep take over. She knew they were going to need rest before they set off again in a few hours. Right now, there were things that mattered and things that didn't. Under different circumstances, she'd have been thrilled by Gage's reaction to her—because she was definitely into him—but nothing about now was normal. She was filing this under Things That Didn't Matter.

* * *

Gage told himself to let go of Nova, to simply get up and put some distance between them. That would be the sane thing. The smart thing. Apparently he was neither of those.

Sometime in the last few hours she'd turned, and now had her leg thrown over his waist as she burrowed into his chest. And he loved it even as it tortured him.

Slowly, Gage moved his hips back, not wanting to embarrass himself further if she woke up. They'd been in a plane crash and apparently not even that could stop his damn dick. Maybe she would forget his reaction to her last night?

Right. He nearly snorted. There was no reason she would, but a man could hope.

He needed to think of something besides Nova. Not the way she was snuggled against him, or the way her vanilla-and-cookies scent lingered in the air. Not the feel of all those lush curves pressed up against him. She was soft in all the right places, but there was a strength to her that he knew was from her yoga and Krav Maga. Holding her like this gave him stupid thoughts.

He hadn't slept much the past few hours, but he had gotten in some solid rest. Sometimes that was all his body needed. Downtime. *Thank you, Marine Corps, for all those years of not sleeping.* His body was trained for the worst situations.

Luckily, they hadn't been disturbed by any wild animals, though that was likely because of the fire, which he'd been adding wood to the last few hours. And potentially the location. They were close enough to maybe not civilization, but some type of residence. He just had to find the damn place he'd seen before they'd crashed. Hell, maybe the owner had seen the plane going down and called the authorities.

And at that thought, he shifted back slightly again—and froze when Nova's dark eyes popped open.

She gave him a soft, sleepy smile as she slid her fingers up his chest. She looked half awake as she leaned toward him, as if she was going to kiss him. Then she blinked and pulled back. "Morning," she murmured, burying her face against his chest.

As if it was the most natural thing to do. She also didn't remove her leg from around him.

"I didn't imagine that plane crash, huh?" she murmured against him.

A short laugh escaped. "Unfortunately no."

For some stupid reason, he kept his arm draped around her waist instead of moving back and getting up. Because he couldn't stop touching her and she wasn't pulling back either. Not really. She had to be sore, and her knee would bother her. Not to mention nothing could ever, ever happen between them. But he still liked holding her.

Groaning, Nova lifted her head and looked at him. "Well, we didn't get eaten by bears, so at least that's something."

"We're more likely to be attacked by a mountain lion than a bear."

She mock smacked his chest. "Really not making me feel any better."

He slid a hand from her waist down to her hip and squeezed tightly. God, he really didn't want to let her go. And having her this close to him was wreaking havoc on all his senses—and body. Which he couldn't quite get under control.

Her breathing hitched slightly and he watched as her eyes dilated. When she licked her lips, he was almost a hundred percent sure that lust flared in her dark eyes.

Nope. This was not a good idea. They were out in the middle of nowhere. He was sort of her boss. She was hurt, dependent on him for protection. He must be seeing things wrong.

So why did he find himself bending his head to hers, brushing his lips over her full, soft ones, as if he had a right to?

She sucked in a breath even as she leaned into him, groaning gently against his mouth.

Oh, hell. He'd wondered what she would sound like if he ever had her in his arms, and this was just the tip of the iceberg. They'd barely kissed and that little moan had his cock pushing even harder against his pants.

When she scooted even closer, she froze as she came in contact with his erection. Then, to his surprise, she rolled her hips against him.

Holy hell. His dick was at full alert now.

No. One of them needed to show some restraint, and he was having a hard time. Though he wanted to do more, it was the last thing in the world they should be doing. Still, he teased the seam of her lips open, gently nibbling on her bottom lip as she arched into him. He could so easily take over, have her flat on her back, strip her pants off and bury his head between her legs. But that wasn't happening. Not here, not now. She deserved better than getting her ass frozen because he couldn't control himself. And...her knee was injured. What the hell was the matter with him?

Breathing hard, he pulled back. "This isn't a good idea."

Reaching between their bodies, she slid her hand over his covered erection, her dark eyes still heavy-lidded. "You sure about that?"

He groaned and rolled his hips against her hand once before going still. "I'm sure," he rasped out. Right? Damn it, he was going to regret this later. But this would screw up everything between them and he couldn't go there. Not with Nova. He wasn't even sure why she was attracted to him. They didn't fit—she was a goddess and he was, well, what the hell ever. He cleared his throat. "How's your knee?" He still held on to her hip, unwilling to break the connection.

She paused, then moved her hand back up to his chest. At least she didn't roll away from him. "It still throbs. Not too bad though. I think when I start moving I'll really feel it."

Though it pained him to do it, he finally pushed up-right, then helped her sit up. She appeared stiff every-where as she shifted and looked around. The sun was rising, but it was still gray and hazy around them.

They were at the bottom of a slope, surrounded by green and brown foliage, mostly some type of fir trees. Behind them were snowcapped mountains—thankfully far in the distance. Now that they could see properly, he could make out what looked like a trail in the distance. Hiking trail maybe. And he could hear running water too. Though there was no way to be sure how far sound traveled in these woods.

Crouching next to her, he gently pushed up her pant leg. She winced slightly, but didn't say anything as he un-wrapped the bandage. The bruising on her knee was worse, but the swelling looked to be about the same.

She bent her leg a little, then stretched it out a couple times. "It hurts but…no worse than a few hours ago. My neck and shoulders are pretty sore though."

"Mine too." Hell, his whole body was sore. Like he'd gone through a few rounds in the ring. "Not much to do about that, unfortunately." And he would take away all her pain if he could. "Though we've got some painkillers in the first aid kit. First…" He pulled two water bottles and protein bars out of the backpack. "Eat and drink."

They were both silent as they devoured the bars and water, and when he was done he checked his phone again. No change. Not that he was surprised.

"You still hungry?" he asked as he handed her two ibuprofen.

"Let's save the food we've got. Just in case."

Not exactly an answer, but she was right. Moving quickly, he rebandaged her knee before standing. "We need to get moving."

She took his outstretched hand and gasped as she stood on both feet. "Maybe I'm more sore than I realized—but I can walk fine." To demonstrate she took a few hobbling steps away from him.

It was definitely going to be slow moving, but that was all right. They were going to get out of here alive. He'd make damn sure of it.

CHAPTER SIX

—Change will always be a part of life. Embrace it.—

As he sat in bed next to his wife, Brooks waited impatiently as his phone rang, again. And again. And again. Colt hadn't answered his damn text and neither had Skye.

Finally Colt picked up on the fourth ring, sounding out of breath. "This better be an emergency."

"The jet never made it to Montana."

There was a moment of silence. "You mean Nova and Gage's flight?"

"Yeah. Jim filed a flight plan, texted me when they left—and hasn't checked in since. According to the private airport, they never made it and I can't get hold of *any* of them. I even tried tracking their phones, but couldn't get a hit." They all had private tracking capabilities in their phones for this very reason. Not being able to contact Nova, Gage or his pilot? This was not good.

"When were they supposed to arrive?"

"About four hours ago. When I woke up, I realized I hadn't gotten a text or email from Gage, and he said he would check in as soon as they'd landed. Before they left, he also said he found some interesting information about some guy Nova had been checking into. But he didn't share anything else." And now Brooks was kicking his own ass for not pushing for more info.

He could practically hear Colt frowning over the phone line. Then he heard Skye in the background say, "Tell him we're on our way home."

"You guys are done with your job?" Skye hadn't said anything last night when he'd talked to her.

"Yep. Finished last night. We'd planned to leave this afternoon but we'll head back now. Have you checked any of the surrounding airports? There are a few private ones within a decent distance of the one they'd planned. Maybe they had to divert because of weather."

"Already checked. And it was a clear night. No weather issues reported anywhere in the vicinity."

Colt cursed.

Brooks always trusted his gut, and it was telling him that something was very wrong right now. If Gage were to go dark, he would have told them beforehand. He wouldn't simply drop off the radar like this. Not only that, but Jim was a civilian. Not one of their crew. There was no way he'd drop off the radar either. "I'm pulling Jim's financials. My dad and I vetted him, but just in case, I'm going to see if anything looks weird on that end." Normally that would be Gage's area of expertise, but they'd have to shift some things around since their resident hacker was unavailable.

"All right. Skye and I will start pulling on some threads on our end too. See if we can dig up anything.

They could be anywhere, especially if the pilot decided to divert the plane."

"Yeah, I was thinking the same thing." Because the only thing Brooks could think of was that the pilot had taken Gage and Nova hostage or...they'd had some kind of technical failure. His jet was new though, so that seemed doubtful. Even so, he couldn't get a hit on the plane's tracking device either. None of this made any sense.

And his spidey sense was going crazy right now. Because there was also the possibility that someone had sabotaged the plane.

None of this was good. "I'll let Savage and Leighton know too." They were currently on jobs, but they needed to be in the loop.

"We'll tell Axel," Colt said.

"Thanks." Axel was engaged to Brooks's baby sister and...okay, he liked the guy. Still, there were some things Brooks was getting used to. Like having a sister at all. He'd only met her less than two years ago. And now she was engaged to a former hit man. Considering Skye was Axel's "best person" in the upcoming nuptials, he was glad Colt had volunteered to contact the man. "I still can't believe you don't care that Skye is now best friends with the guy," he muttered.

Colt just grunted and hung up.

"It's not good, is it?" Darcy said next to him, propped up against the headboard as she watched him, worry clear in her pale green eyes.

"Too soon to tell, but I don't like that we can't get ahold of any of them."

"I'll make some coffee," she said, slipping out of bed, but not before kissing him soundly.

Just like that, his heart rate kicked up, even as he started to call Savage. He wasn't sure what he'd done to deserve Darcy, but he was the luckiest man in the universe.

* * *

"All right, I've come to a decision," Nova rasped out as she leaned against a nearby tree trunk. Even though she desperately wanted to collapse, she forced herself to remain standing.

"What's up? Do you need more water?" Gage didn't look winded at all. Just concerned for her.

Under normal circumstance, she'd be fine. But it had been two hours and they'd gone a little over two miles. Which was pathetic. She could fast-walk two miles in half an hour. Ridiculous. Her knee was killing her though. "I already know you're going to argue with me so let me finish. I'm slowing us down. And I don't want you to abandon me, so just get that out of your head. However, I think you should go ahead and look for help. It's still really early. So if you head out and can't find anything, you can come back and get me long before dark. And we'll set up camp again."

Gage's jaw clenched. "We've been over this. I'm not leaving you."

"And I'm not asking you to. I'm asking you to *save* us. If I could, I would, trust me. I hate being so useless."

"You're not—"

"Gage. Seriously. I'm slowing us down. I'm more than fine to sit here by myself and wait. I might hate it, but I'll do it." As another thought occurred to her, she frowned. "You seem like Superman to me, but maybe I'm misjudging? How are you feeling?" She inwardly winced, feeling guilty for not even factoring that in. Gage simply seemed so invincible and he hadn't mentioned being injured at all. Plus he was moving like a tiger. All sexy, sleek and lethal.

"I'm fine. I just don't like the thought of leaving you here."

"I know you have more than one weapon. Just leave one with me." She might not love weapons, but she was trained with them.

His jaw tightened again and he glanced around the forest, as if looking for answers. They'd been on a trail for a while and it was well-worn so it had to lead somewhere. And if Gage could simply get there, they would be okay. But she was burning daylight they couldn't afford to lose. And it was only going to get worse. The wind was picking up, burning her lungs and making it harder to breathe—which made it even more difficult to walk. She was using up energy she didn't have.

She stepped forward and placed her hands on his chest. "Look, I'm not saying one thing when I mean another, Gage. I seriously mean that I want you to go ahead. I want to get the hell out of these woods and I want to help my friend. The best way to do that is if you go ahead. So stop beating yourself up because I can see that you're doing it."

Sighing, he laid his forehead against hers. "I hate the thought of leaving you alone." The words were torn from his chest, and they warmed her deep inside.

This man was going to kill her with all this protectiveness. She really adored him. She wrapped her arms around him and buried her face against his chest. "Once you find help, maybe we can finish what we started," she murmured, even as her cheeks heated up. It was a bold thing to say, especially for her. Yeah, she was outgoing and an extrovert, but Gage could seriously break her heart. And she was putting herself out there. She had no idea if he regretted what had happened before. Or if he'd just been caught up in the moment and wanted nothing more from her.

He groaned. "You fight dirty."

Startled, she laughed and looked up at him to find his expression filled with lust as he watched her with those pale, bluish-gray eyes. She started to say something about the word dirty, but snapped her mouth shut. She needed to focus on getting him to listen to her—to go get help.

"I'll be back for you before dark. If I don't find help, I'm returning. If I'm not back before dark, start the fire and stay close to it. And keep my weapon on you at all times." He was already opening his backpack as he started talking, once again going into straight business mode.

"I can do all of that. And I'll keep heading down this trail. I won't diverge from it." She could still walk a little, but she'd be moving slowly. Though she figured she only had another hour in her right now. Her knee throbbed and she felt as if she could sleep for a year.

He paused as he pulled out his extra SIG. "I'm going on the record again as saying I hate this. I *hate* leaving you."

Going on instinct, she leaned forward and brushed her mouth over his when he stood.

He seemed startled by the action but slightly deepened the kiss, teasing her tongue with his. She wanted to lean into him, wrap her body around him and… Yeah, none of these thoughts were helpful so it was a good thing he pulled back. Though it made her happy that he groaned as he did.

It didn't take long for him to get his stuff together. With his weapon tucked into his holster, he grabbed a couple bottles of water and energy bars but he left almost everything with her, including the backpack. When she started to protest, he shook his head.

"The backpack will slow me down. Trust me, I've survived on a lot less for longer. I'm going to head down this trail as far as possible. If in four hours I haven't found any signs of life, I'm headed back." He glanced at his watch. "That way I'll be back in plenty of time before dark. Don't move from this path if you decide to keep going. Promise."

"I promise." She really hoped Gage found help before then. Otherwise she was stuck sitting here for eight hours alone. And she really hated that she wasn't able to help more. She felt completely useless. "And thank you," she said quietly.

He didn't respond, just kissed her again in a harsh, demanding claiming that took her completely off guard and left her lips swollen and tingling.

Then he was gone, jogging down the trail at a steady pace. She knew he ran for exercise, and that he was into martial arts. If anyone was going to find help, it was Gage. Though she hated watching him go, she prayed that he found help. And that she'd still be able to get to Layla in time.

At that thought, she pulled her cell phone out and looked at it. Yep. Still no service.

Not a surprise, but seeing the X where the service bars should be just brought her mood down even more. Instead of following the trail, she decided to sit for a bit and try to recharge.

And wait.

* * *

Nova leaned on the long wooden stick she was using as a makeshift crutch. If she had to guess, she'd gone maybe half a mile. And she was pretty sure she was over-estimating. Which just felt pathetic, considering she'd been walking *an hour*.

Out of habit, she dug into her backpack and checked her phone to see if she had service. No such luck. Still that same stupid X where the bars should be. She hoped Gage was having better luck than her. But of course he would be; the man was like a machine.

She was so incredibly grateful he was with her right now, even if not in the technical, physical sense. For more reasons than just one. He'd gotten under her skin and wasn't going anywhere. She'd never imagined this sort of chemistry with anyone, and with him it was like electricity simply arced between them. Had been like that since they'd met. At least on her end. He joked around with her, and pseudo-flirted, but until last night and that impressive erection? She hadn't been sure how he felt about her.

After shoving her phone back inside her pack, she pulled out one of the water bottles. But she only took a few sips. She knew without a doubt that Gage would come back for her, but she was also a realist. *Anything* could happen to him and she had to conserve her re-sources. Unfortunately, she couldn't conserve her en-ergy. Not when it was taking all she had to stumble down this dirt pathway.

At least it was fairly worn. Little patches of grass had grown in certain areas, though the foliage was now brown because it was fall. But it hadn't completely grown over, which meant it got some use—so there had to be other humans somewhere around here.

Wherever here was.

One step at a time, she reminded herself. One step, then another. She had to focus on that and not the throbbing ache in her knee.

She continued onward, her steps small, the wind cutting into her lungs with every breath she took. When it became too much, she decided to take another break and leaned against a nearby tree.

As she slumped to the hard earth, she realized she'd never noticed how much she took for granted having her phone, or her e-reader, or some form of entertainment. On top of being in pain and stranded in the middle of nowhere, she was a little bored. She was tired of being lost in her own thoughts, mainly because all she did was stress about Gage and his sexy ass—and he did have a fine butt. She was having way too many fantasies about how nice it would be to nibble on it. God, she needed to get it together and stop daydreaming about him. And his ass.

When she heard a rustling somewhere nearby, she groaned and started to push up to her feet again. It seemed doubtful, but maybe there were hunters or something out here. And maybe they would have a satellite phone—and an ATV. A woman could hope.

She froze when she heard a low, threatening growl.

Blindly, she reached for her backpack. Unzipping it, she pulled out the SIG that Gage had given her.

There was another growl, this time closer.

"Please don't be a stupid bear," she muttered as she steadied her weapon. She really didn't want to shoot any animal, but she was also pretty sure that a bullet wouldn't do much to stop a bear. Those giant mammoths seemed indestructible.

When everything around her went silent, the rush of blood in her ears was like a raging river. Movement in the corner of her eye snagged her attention.

Then she really, *really* wished she was anywhere but here as a huge mountain lion stalked onto the pathway. Its movements were lethal, predatory.

Ice trickled down her spine, her hands going clammy as she stared at the beautiful animal. Yeah, she really didn't want to shoot it. But if it came down to her or it, she was taking the shot.

As it started trotting down the pathway toward her, she forced herself to stand straighter, ignoring the ache in her leg as she did. Using the tree as leverage, she leaned against it. "Get out of here!" she shouted. She'd read somewhere that making yourself look bigger and being loud was supposed to help scare away animals. Maybe that didn't apply to these kinds of predators though?

She swore if she ever got home, she was going to read up on all of that survivalist shit.

The animal stilled, its body tensing as it stared her down. So she shouted again. "I really don't want to shoot you! Get out of here!"

It let out the creepiest sounding roar.

Another rustling sounded nearby, and her heart rate jacked up about a thousand notches. What the hell? Did mountain lions travel in packs? She didn't think so. It would totally be her luck if another one showed up.

And she was the perfect prey: a nice afternoon snack that could barely walk, let alone run away. Not that she'd have a chance of outrunning this thing on her best day.

More movement caught her gaze.

When a sleek, beautiful deer stepped onto the dirt path, her eyes widened.

The deer paused for only a second. Then it was off, the doe darting back into the trees lightning fast.

Nova forgotten, the mountain lion gave chase, moving so fast and so quietly, his body pure, raw beauty. It made her realize she should have kept her weapon up and on it the whole time. Because it moved *fast*.

So...that had just happened.

Trembling, she put her backpack on, but kept the gun at her side as she hobbled down the path. No way was she taking a break now.

She knew the animal could smell her if it wanted to track her, but she wasn't sticking around here any longer. She was going to go as far as she could until her body gave out.

And pray that the mountain lion didn't change his mind about the deer and come after her instead.

CHAPTER SEVEN

—Good friends are like stars. You don't always see
them, but you know they're always there.—

"You're gonna be in a hell of a lot of trouble if you're
lying," Elijah Kavanagh, the man driving the Gator, muttered as they headed down the riding trail.

Gage wanted to tell the old man to hurry up. He also
wanted to ask the rancher what kind of dumbass would
lie about a plane crash? He could have come up with a
better lie, like he and his friend got lost hiking. But he'd
been honest, because sometimes honesty really was best.
Since the man was taking him to get Nova, he kept his
temper in check.

"Look. You've got my weapon." Well, technically
Gage had surrendered it in good faith—none of the men
at that ranch he'd found could have taken it from him.
"And we've called the local PD. I'm not lying. Can this
thing go any faster?"

Elijah simply nodded and increased his speed a bit.
Not enough, in Gage's opinion, but it would have to do.
He'd been on that trail about an hour and a half when
he'd run into some cowboys fixing a fence. By then he'd
been exhausted, and they hadn't been too happy to see
his holstered weapon or him so far onto private ranching

land. So he'd been honest, and now here he was, with the owner of Kavanagh Ranch, headed to get Nova.

He looked at his watch again. She'd been alone only a little over two hours by now. She should be okay. He forced every single horrible scenario out of his head and focused on simply getting to her. "You tell the cops to bring an ambulance?" Or whatever the hell they had out here.

"I told the sheriff that we might have a medical situation." He still sounded skeptical, but that was all right. Because Gage had called Brooks when he'd had service back at the ranch. He didn't anymore, not on this damn trail, but Brooks at least knew what had happened and would be getting someone else involved in this whole mess.

Because Gage didn't trust the locals to handle the autopsy of the pilot. And no matter what, he wanted that body autopsied. He hadn't seen any signs of foul play, but something had to have happened to Jim.

"There she is!" All the muscles in Gage's body tightened as he spotted Nova propped up against a tree, one leg stretched out, her head tilted back slightly and her eyes closed. She was about a mile closer than where he'd left her.

She didn't even stir at their approach and panic lit inside him like a wildfire. He jumped out of the Gator before Elijah had fully stopped.

The man muttered something but Gage ignored him. "Nova!" His boots kicked up dust as he rushed down the last few feet of the trail.

Blinking, she opened her eyes and watched him in confusion for a moment. The SIG was held loosely in her hand at her side and she'd braided her long dark hair. Despite the fatigue in her eyes, she was as stunning as ever. "Gage?" She blinked again, rolling her neck once. "You..." She trailed off, looking past him, no doubt at the Gator and Elijah.

"I found help and I've called Brooks. By the time we get back to Elijah's ranch, law enforcement should be there with questions." Reaching out, he gently helped her to her feet and took the weapon, immediately holstering it.

She practically collapsed into him, but her grip was strong. "I'm so glad you're back."

"Nothing could have kept me away."

To Gage's surprise, Elijah stepped up, a soft smile on his face. "Hi, ma'am, let me help you." He took Nova's other arm and helped steady her as they headed back to the vehicle. "I'm going to apologize in advance for the bumpy ride. Your friend here told me you hurt your knee."

"It's okay. I just appreciate you helping us. I'm Nova, by the way." Her voice was a little thready, as if she was fighting exhaustion.

Which she clearly was. He just hoped the only thing wrong was her knee, not something internal. He wanted to pull her into his arms, to hold her close. But the ATV was only a two-seater so he helped her get settled in the passenger seat then jumped into the back hatch. Even though Elijah hadn't believed Gage about the plane crash, he'd still brought water and food, which he immediately offered to Nova.

The old man was a hell of a lot nicer to *her* than he'd been to Gage. Which was a good thing. For how raw he was feeling, Gage wasn't going to put up with any shit right now. The man could be suspicious of him all he wanted but he'd better treat her with respect.

"What kind of ranch do you own?" Nova asked before taking a small sip of her water.

Gage winced at every bump they hit, hating that she had to be so uncomfortable right now.

"Cattle. Horses." A short, succinct answer, not that Gage was surprised. "Tell me about y'all. Where were you headed?"

"Billings. On a private jet owned by the company we work for. I still…can't believe what happened." Nova's voice broke on the last word, and that seemed to have an effect on the old man.

Gage knew he'd just been asking her to see if their stories matched. Or at least that's what he guessed Elijah had been doing. Now, however, the rancher just patted her arm and told her to sit back and rest.

Gage couldn't rest, and wouldn't, not until he had Nova somewhere safe. Until someone could check her out thoroughly and make sure she wasn't injured worse than they thought.

She cleared her throat once. "I saw a mountain lion. Thought I might have to shoot it but a deer distracted it." Sighing, she covered her face with her hands. "I can't believe I fell asleep back there."

He heard the fear in her voice even as it invaded his own veins. Hell, mountain lions were fast and vicious. If she'd been sleeping, it could have attacked and done maximum damage so damn quickly. He fought off a shudder. Reaching forward, he squeezed her shoulder once. "You're okay now."

She lifted a hand, and though she didn't turn in her seat, she covered his hand with hers and squeezed.

That simple action made his chest tighten. He wished he'd been with her. If anything had happened to her... *Nope.* Not going there.

* * *

Nova let out a small breath of relief as the sheriff stepped out of Elijah Kavanagh's kitchen, giving her and Gage privacy. Not much, but enough. She was simply glad to be alone with Gage again. Or semi-alone.

They hadn't had a moment alone together since they'd arrived at the ranch because Sheriff Lydia Olsen had already been waiting. The tall blonde with the pixie cut and pale blue eyes was a little intimidating. At least to Nova. Gage had his neutral mask in place and had answered everything professionally.

She, on the other hand, had gotten a little teary when talking about the crash and felt like a jackass. "I can't believe I started crying when she was questioning me," Nova muttered low enough for only Gage to hear.

Frowning, he reached over and took her hand in his, sliding his fingers through hers. "Your reaction is normal. We've been through a lot and your brain is probably just catching up with everything and digesting the reality of it."

"You seem totally fine." He was taking everything in stride, to the point where she felt like a hot mess.

He lifted a shoulder, and she remembered that he'd been in multiple war zones. Of course he would be better able to handle everything. Still, she hated that she felt as if she was barely hanging on.

Still exhausted, she'd declined going to a hospital. Especially since the nearest one was about fifty miles away. Apparently they really were in the middle of nowhere. And it would take a solid eight, potentially nine hours of driving to get to Billings. They certainly weren't going this afternoon. She was supposed to meet Layla tomorrow but they might not make it until the evening. Nova didn't trust herself enough to drive, and she knew that Gage had to be exhausted even if he was hiding it well. Besides, she wasn't certain the sheriff was going to let them go anyway.

The sheriff was talking to someone in the other room, clearly on the phone or her radio, speaking in hushed tones. It was impossible to hear what the other woman was saying. And Nova was almost too tired to care. But too many things were racing through her mind. She wondered what they were going to do about the plane, and more importantly, Jim. His body needed to be retrieved, and he would have to be transported back to South Carolina. And someone would have to notify his family.

At that thought, more tears welled up but she quickly blinked them away. As she did, the sheriff stepped back into the kitchen, Elijah with her.

The rancher didn't pay attention to any of them as he went to the half-full coffeepot and poured himself a mug. Without asking, he refreshed her mug and Gage's. She gave him a grateful smile even as the sheriff started talking. It was a little late for coffee, but the warmth spread through her.

"One of you has some powerful friends," the sheriff said, looking between the two of them. "The Feds are going to send two people in to help with the retrieval of the pilot and handle the autopsy. They sent me a satellite image from the coordinates you gave me. Seems you're telling the truth, and I'm sorry for what you've been through." She continued talking for the next couple minutes, and Nova paid attention as best she could but she was fading fast. She caught all the important parts, including the fact that they would have to talk to the

Feds later, but they weren't being held on charges or suspicion.

What the hell could the cops hold them for anyway? Surviving a plane crash? Gage had been flying with two weapons, and she wasn't sure he was allowed to, but Elijah hadn't said anything about his SIGs. And Nova certainly wasn't going to offer up that information either.

When Gage stood, Nova realized the sheriff was done talking. She stood as well and nodded politely at the other woman, even as her knee twinged in discomfort.

Sheriff Olsen shook Nova's hand, then Gage's once. "I can give you a ride anywhere you want to go."

"Don't worry about that," Elijah said, his thick drawl coming through even more now. "I'm going to get the two of them squared away. Besides, the nearest motel is about an hour away. They're in no shape to go anywhere. You know I've got the space."

Nova was ready to get out of there even if the man was right, but Gage simply nodded his agreement. So she did too. Maybe he'd worked something out with the rancher?

"Suit yourself. But call me if y'all need anything. I'll see myself out." The sheriff nodded at Elijah and said something about seeing him at church that Sunday.

The rancher simply grunted, and once they were alone he said, "I talked to that friend of yours, Brooks Alexander. He called me while you were being questioned by Lydia. Told me to make sure you were taken care of and that he'd pay for me to take you to a rental car place once you've had some rest."

Nova wondered how the heck Brooks had gotten the man's number, but then remembered Gage had said he'd spoken to Brooks earlier. "That's incredibly kind, thank you."

The older man shrugged. "It's kind but also selfish. We're going to do some business together."

"We are?" She frowned.

Gage laughed lightly and wrapped an arm around her shoulders. "He means him and Brooks."

Oh, right. Brooks might be one of the cofounders of Redemption Harbor Consulting, but he also had a bunch of other businesses as well, including ranching. Clearly her brain wasn't functioning at full capacity. Hell, not even half. Yeah, getting on the road right now was not a good idea. She'd already texted Layla a few times and knew her friend was okay for now, so at least she could rest easy about that. Well, as much as possible. She wouldn't rest until she saw Layla for herself and helped her out of whatever situation she was in.

"I've got more than a few spare bedrooms here, or y'all can bunk at one of the cabins. I've got two empty right now and—"

"Cabin is fine. We want to head out early, if that's not a problem," Gage said.

"Early as you want. Let me get some food together so y'all have something to eat." And that was that.

The thought of a hot shower—maybe with Gage—was the only thing keeping her going right now. Her knee was in pain, but if Gage was finally ready to give in to the attraction simmering between them, nothing would stop her.

CHAPTER EIGHT

—You only regret the chances you don't take.—

"Maybe we should have stayed in the main house," Nova muttered, looking around the sparse cabin. Clearly it had been furnished by a man.

There was an old-looking plaid couch, and a solid wood coffee table in front of it that looked as if it had been beaten up with cowboy boots—possibly with spurs on them. There was also a television so old she hadn't realized they were still around—and a VHS player next to it. Also something she hadn't thought anyone used anymore.

The cabin was small, with only one bedroom, an attached bathroom, and the kitchen and living room were basically one giant room with no divider except for different flooring. Wood for the living room and tile for the cute country kitchen.

Gage just grunted and started getting the fireplace prepped. At least the house was clean and would be warm soon—once Gage got the fire going. She'd turned the heat on, but it was taking its sweet time warming things up. She shouldn't be complaining, not even in her head. Because she was alive.

The truth was, she was simply nervous about being alone with Gage. They'd kissed a couple times, but now what? They were back to the real world. Well, sort of the real world. Because as soon as they got a few hours of sleep, they'd be heading out and it would be game on. She had no time in her life for any entanglements.

Okay, that was just an excuse. She was nervous about what Gage made her feel. She'd had boyfriends, but things had always been casual. And she'd *always* been the one to break things off.

She'd never had her heart broken. Because she'd never cared enough about a guy for him to matter. When she worked for the CIA, dating had been out. And in college, she definitely hadn't bothered because all she'd cared about was graduating and getting a job—getting as far away from the life she'd known as possible. When you grew up poor, priorities shifted. And boys? No, they hadn't factored into her life at all. Stability and money were what had mattered.

Once she'd started working for who she now thought of as Mr. Corporate Douchebag, she'd actually had time in her life to date. Only she hadn't been too impressed with what was out there.

And deep down, she knew Gage could seriously break her heart. Okay, it wasn't even very deep down. She *knew* he could. He was so damn smart and it was impossible to read him at times. He had this cute little tell when he was lying about something, but sometimes his expression went completely neutral and she couldn't read *anything* from him. So when he'd crushed his mouth over hers before he'd gone for help, she'd felt it all the way to her core.

And she'd thought about it right up until she'd passed out against a tree. Well, she'd been thinking about that kiss and also worried about mountain lions. Not worried enough, apparently, because she'd still fallen asleep.

"What's wrong?" Gage asked as he stood up from the fireplace.

She blinked, surprised to see little flames already dancing. That was when she realized she was just standing there, holding her backpack and doing nothing. She set it on the kitchen table and cleared her throat. "Honestly, I'm just kind of spacing out."

He nodded, as if he completely understood. "I'll take the couch and you can sleep in the bedroom."

Okay, that wasn't what she'd expected him to say. "You want to sleep on the couch?"

"I'll sleep on the damn floor. I don't care. Your knee is injured and you're taking the bed, so don't argue with me."

She hadn't *planned* on arguing with him, but she was incredibly disappointed he didn't want to join her. What the hell? She'd thought…

Clearly it didn't matter what she'd thought. He wasn't on the same wavelength. For a brief moment she contemplated inviting him to join her, but she didn't have the mental energy to deal with a rejection right now.

"Okay. Ah...I guess I'll take a shower, then. Unless you want to take one now?"

He shook his head. "I'll make us some sandwiches. Elijah gave us enough to whip up something decent tonight. And we both need to eat."

"Okay, thanks." After she shut the door, she leaned against it and closed her eyes. Part of her wanted to go out there and ask him to join her, but again, she did *not* have any sort of capacity to deal with a rejection right now.

After laying out clean clothes, she stripped and made her way to the shower. It took a while to warm up but she was so grateful once she finally stepped underneath the spray. Elijah had said there was shampoo and stuff here, but it was basic stuff from the dollar store. And she didn't care that she was using V05 instead of her ridiculous sulfate-free, twenty-dollar shampoo, because her hair was clean and she finally felt human again.

As she washed her body with the vanilla-scented wash, her hand strayed between her legs for a long moment as she thought about Gage. Tall, sexy, frustrating man.

He had her all twisted up inside. He'd kissed her more than once when they'd been out in the wild, and he'd been into it. She'd felt his reaction clearly.

As she started to tease her clit, she felt almost...not guilty, but a little weird. It would be so easy to get herself off in here, but with him in the next room? Yeah, it just felt too weird.

Feeling edgy and frustrated, she quickly finished up, and though she hated turning off the hot water, she wanted to make sure there was enough left for Gage. But when she finished, she realized she'd completely forgotten to get a towel. Damn it.

After quickly searching the small bathroom, she discovered there weren't any in here either. "Of course not," she muttered to herself.

Dripping wet and annoyed at this point because that wonderful warmth was gone and she was freezing her ass off, she cracked open the bedroom door. "Can you see if there are any towels out there?"

There was a short pause. "Yeah." Thankfully, less than a minute later, he shoved a handful of towels through the door.

She shut it behind her and cursed her own cowardice. Now would be the perfect time to…

What? Invite him in? She groaned. She was such an idiot. He was a pretty alpha guy. If he wanted something, he'd go for it.

Chilled now, she quickly wrapped her hair in a towel and dried off. She needed sleep, not to be focusing on Gage and how annoyingly sexy he was. And she definitely didn't need to think about the fact that he would be naked and in the shower soon himself.

Nope. Not thinking about that at all.

* * *

Gage hurriedly dried off after stepping out of the shower. He could have taken a longer one, but he wanted to get back to Nova. When she'd come out of the bedroom in skintight yoga pants—or whatever they were—and a fitted T-shirt with no bra, he'd had to force himself to look anywhere but at her. The woman took his breath away...and made him hard as stone.

He'd jerked off in the shower thinking about her. Which wasn't completely out of the realm of normal for him. He was *always* thinking about her. He'd felt a little bad doing it with her in the next room, but it was better than coming out here with his dick hard.

When he stepped out of the bedroom, he found her sitting on the couch, drinking...a glass of red wine?

She lifted the glass and grinned. "Elijah brought a bottle over. Said it was his deceased wife's and figured we deserved it after surviving a plane crash. I happily accepted."

Laughing lightly, he headed to the kitchen, which was only a few steps from the living room. "I'm actually going to have one too."

"I thought I was ready to crash but I could stay up and watch TV for a bit. The shower really refreshed me. Unless you're tired, then I'll hit the bed now."

He could easily crash, but it was only six. He wasn't certain how that was possible when it felt as if he'd lived a hundred years in the last twenty-four hours. "TV's fine. Did you eat?" he asked, even as he opened the fridge to grab some cheese.

"Yeah, thanks for making the sandwich."

It was on the tip of his tongue to tell her he'd cook real food for her when they got home, but he held off. The few kisses they'd shared…they couldn't happen again. For so many reasons. He was her boss. Fuck. Her *boss*. Nope. Not going down that road. Not to mention he'd been there, done that, gotten his heart broken before.

And Nova? She meant more to him than any woman ever had. And they were simply friends. *Fuuuck.* If he lost her? No. Just, no. He couldn't even imagine that. He wouldn't. It would take time, but they would go back to normal.

She seemed fine when he'd said he'd sleep out here, so he was probably just overthinking shit for no reason. Everything had been intense earlier; they'd both done things they regretted.

Okay, that was a lie. He regretted nothing. And he wanted more of her.

So. Much. More.

But that wasn't happening. He just needed to remind himself of that. "Have you heard from Layla again?" he asked, sitting on the opposite end of the couch.

"Yeah." She motioned to her phone on the beat-up coffee table. "She said she decided to head to the spa early and will see me tomorrow. She was worried about my knee, but I told her it was no big deal."

"How *is* your knee?"

"Not bad. Sore...like the rest of me." Her leg was stretched out in front of her on the coffee table, an ace bandage wrapped around a pack of ice he'd found in the freezer earlier.

"That can't be comfortable. Here, just put it on me." Apparently, he liked playing with fire. Grabbing a pillow, he put it on his lap. "The elevation should help too."

"You sure? I didn't want to be a couch hog." Her expression was neutral as she watched him. She'd braided her damp hair so that it hung over her shoulder.

God, what he wouldn't give to unbraid it, run his fingers through it as he claimed her mouth again. "It's fine. Trust me. So what are we watching?"

"Well, he doesn't have Netflix or anything so...our two VHS choices were *Care Bears* and *The Goonies*. I think you can guess which one I chose."

He barked out a laugh even as he took her sock-covered foot in his hand. He shouldn't touch her. But yeah, he was really playing with fire. "This okay?" he asked, softly massaging the bottom of her foot.

She nodded once, took a sip of her wine before turning on the movie. He was vaguely aware of the characters on screen, but all his focus was on Nova, even if he wasn't looking at her.

She let out a little moan when he kneaded her arch. So he did it again. He was glad he had a pillow on his lap.

"Why'd you leave your last job?" She'd never told him, and he was curious why she'd left the job she'd had before coming to work for Redemption Harbor Consulting.

Skye had once made a comment to him about Nova leaving because her boss had been a jerk, but Nova had been tightlipped about it—and "a jerk" could have meant so many things.

"That's random," she murmured, giving him a sleepy smile.

Hell, he'd probably be carrying her to the bed soon. He deserved a medal if he could leave her there and walk away. "I'm curious."

"I'll tell you if you tell me why you got into hacking."

"I did it to impress a girl. I was fourteen and stupid. And I still didn't get the girl. But I did manage to hack into our school's system and change her grade."

Nova blinked as a grin spread across her face. "Fourteen?"

"Yeah. They caught the error—not me, thankfully—and it got changed back."

"You really are a bad boy."

The sultry way she said that had his dick going even harder. She was clearly trying to kill him. "Fair's fair. Why'd you leave?"

She rolled her eyes, but he saw the hurt that flickered there. It put him on alert, but he kept up the soft massage of her foot.

"My boss was great. Or, I thought he was great. Very professional. We had strict boundaries for what I did, how many hours I worked, I had great benefits, and I genuinely loved what I did. It was very fast-paced and he always had my back. And…I'm just stalling." She let out a shaky breath and took another sip of wine. It seemed to steady her.

"I'm not going anywhere." He almost regretted asking her, but this was what he wanted from Nova. He wanted all of her. The real, unfiltered version.

"I was in my boss's office, getting some stuff ready for a meeting he was having. I wasn't attending because I hated the guy he was meeting with. Such a creeper. He'd never done anything outright but I didn't like him, and my boss never pushed back when I asked if it was necessary for me to be there. So…long story short, the guy arrived early and my boss was late. He tried to hurt me. Would have… Hell, I don't know *what* he wanted. Not completely. But he was stupid to think he could have gotten away with it." She let out a bitter-sounding laugh and muttered, "Or maybe not. Anyway, he had me shoved up against a wall, had ripped my shirt down the front and would have hurt me. The cops would have been involved—*should* have been involved—I had bruises on my neck, to give you some details. But my boss came in and freaked out. Punched the guy. In that moment, I knew everything would be okay. Or I assumed it would be. As soon as the asshole was escorted out by security, I picked up the phone, ready to call the cops. But…my boss stopped me. And he'd told security to hold off. I only found that out later."

Gage's jaw tightened, already hating where this was going. "Why?"

"Because the asshole—that's what I call him—was a big client. They needed him and didn't want the scandal."

"Fuck."

"Yeah, that about sums it up. I was pissed. But more than that, I was hurt. My boss...I thought he respected me. I'd been to his house before, knew his wife. Adored her, actually. I'd been to his kids' birthday parties. And he wanted me to take one for the team." Now her laugh wasn't bitter, just sad.

And Gage seriously wanted to punch shit. To take all her pain away.

"I...I'm ashamed that I didn't push back harder. Maybe I should have. But, honestly, it was self-preservation. At heart, I'm a realist. The guy who'd attacked me, he wouldn't have gone down quietly. I could see my face getting splashed across the news, people calling me an attention whore, or simply a whore, whatever. I could actually see how it would play out, my entire life being dredged up and inspected for public consumption. Considering I used to work for the CIA? Noooo. I wasn't going down that path. I had no doubt that the man who'd attacked me would hire lawyers and do a public smear campaign. He would have destroyed my reputation.

"So I told my boss to eat shit. That he was going to pay me six months' severance and HR was going to write me a glowing letter of reference. I asked for some other things...and I got them. Then I backed up a bunch of files I most definitely shouldn't have, and I left. The sad thing is, they ended up losing in the long run. The asshole went to jail for embezzling from his own company."

Damn. That was not what he'd expected. "Is that why you take Krav Maga?"

"Yeah. I never wanted to feel so vulnerable again."

Good. "What's his name?"

Her dark eyes widened. "Uh-uh. I'm not telling you—and it's why I didn't mention any names when I was telling you all this. Look, he's not a terrible guy. I mean...I guess he is. But I'm not letting you rip his life apart because of this. He's got two little girls and a wife. Leave him alone."

"Not him. The other one. The one who laid his hands on you." The man who Gage felt like ripping limb from limb. Slowly. Savagely.

She blinked again in that adorable way of hers then shifted away from him, pulling her foot back. "No way. You don't get to use those magic fingers and try to distract me. I'm not telling you anything."

Magic fingers, huh? He made a mental note about that. "I can find out on my own."

"Then find out on your own. I'm not telling you." She gave him a haughty look that shouldn't have been so sexy.

Shouldn't have turned him on as much as it did. Well, turned him on even more. Because his dick was rock-hard. "Why?"

"Because I don't want you to go to jail for homicide, and you look a little homicidal right now."

He was glad she cared. Still... "I wouldn't get caught."

"See? That stuff right there? That's why I'm not telling you. I can't tell if you're serious or not."

He just shrugged because he wasn't sure either. Someone had attacked Nova. Laid hands on her. Ripped her clothes, bruised her. No, he could *not* think about that now. Even if he never touched the guy, he'd make sure the man suffered.

"Besides, he's in jail anyway. He's not getting out for a looooong time." She snorted derisively. "The *really* sad part is, if he'd gone to jail for assaulting me—which he likely wouldn't have—he'd have done a lot less time than what he got caught for. So there, now you know why I left."

"Your ex-boss is a dick."

"I know. He did apologize later. Or he tried to. He called me a few times, sent emails, an actual gift basket. Like a basket of chocolate and wine would make up for him stabbing me in the back. I don't know if he actually was sorry, but I like to think he regretted what he did." She shrugged and turned back to the television. "It was a wake-up call, that's for sure."

Gage wasn't sure what she meant by that and decided not to push. "I didn't mean to upset you," he murmured, hating that he'd even asked her now.

Surprising him, she turned and gave him a small smile. "It's okay. I'm glad you know, and I'm not upset."

He didn't know what to make of that, either, so he simply nodded and turned back to the TV. The entire situation might suck, but he liked spending time with her away from everyone.

Leaning back against the ugly but comfortable couch, he kicked his own feet up on the sturdy table and tried to pay attention to the movie.

Next to him, Nova laid her head on a pillow and curled up as she attempted to watch the movie too. But she was out in less than twenty minutes. No wonder. Hell, he was ready to get some sleep too.

But first he stepped outside and called Brooks, then Skye, who was of course with Colt. They'd already told everyone else what was going on, and since everyone had either wrapped up or was in the process of wrapping up current jobs, soon they'd all be back in Redemption Harbor. And Leighton had really come through by getting Hazel—a special agent with the FBI—to send in a couple of her people to check out the plane crash. They'd done the Feds more than one favor. They owed Redemption Harbor Consulting. Even if those favors had been off the books.

Once he was done, he found Nova still sleeping on the couch, the TV off. For a long moment, he looked down at her, feeling... Hell, he wasn't sure what he felt around her. He rubbed the middle of his chest, but that ache didn't go away as he looked at her long eyelashes fanning over her cheekbones. Nothing could happen between them. He knew it even if he hated it. She was vulnerable right now and he could never, ever be the guy who hurt her.

Time to get her to bed.

She stirred slightly as he scooped her up in his arms. She was tall and lean and fit perfectly against him. "What are you doing?" she murmured, curling into him.

"Movie's over. I'm putting you in bed." Unfortunately, he wouldn't be sharing it with her.

"Stay with me," she murmured, nuzzling her face against his chest.

Hell. "That's not a good idea."

She was silent until he made it to the bedroom and laid her on the bed. It was queen-size, so more than big enough for the two of them.

"I just don't want to be alone tonight." Her eyes were closed as she curled on her side away from him.

Dammit. There was no way he could walk away from that. So he slid into bed and wrapped his arms around her. Pulling her close, he felt at peace for the first time in ages. Simply holding her was cathartic. They could talk in the morning about "them." Or rather, what they weren't and could never be. Just because nothing physical could happen between the two of them didn't mean they couldn't be friends.

Hell, her friendship was one of the most important things in his life. He couldn't give it up. He couldn't give *her* up.

When she shifted in her sleep, her tight ass rubbed right over his cock.

He gritted his teeth, already cursing his decision to do this. It was the sweetest form of torture: holding the woman he'd fallen for and could never have.

CHAPTER NINE

—Know your worth. Then add tax.—

Nova couldn't fight the energy humming through her as they neared Billings. The spa actually wasn't in the city but on the outskirts in an exclusive resort. "It's Layla," she said to Gage, answering her phone on the second ring. "Hey, girl," she said, injecting excitement into her voice. It was better than fear.

"Hey! Are you close? I can't wait to see you." Layla sounded normal enough but that meant nothing.

Nova knew that much. They were both experienced at wearing masks and blending in when they needed to. "I should be there in the next hour. I'm so sorry for the delay. Luckily I won't have to do much at the spa," she said, laughing lightly, as if she didn't have a care in the world.

"No problem. What happened to your knee?"

Nova had been vague on the details and she was going to continue to be vague—and not tell her friend that she'd been in a plane crash. Not yet anyway. It would invite too many questions, and if her fiancé got wind of it, it might look odd that she was still continuing on to the spa. "Oh, you know me, I'm so clumsy. It's ridiculous. Where should I meet you when I get there?"

Layla cleared her throat. "Well, my fiancé surprised me and wanted to join us for dinner tonight. There's a great restaurant on site. How does seven o'clock sound? Will that give you enough time to freshen up?"

Nova didn't miss a beat. "That's perfect. I'll have just enough time to shower and get ready. Can't wait to see you and to meet this mystery man of yours." A man she wanted to throat punch.

Once they disconnected, she relayed the plans to Gage. "Her fiancé is there."

His fingers tightened slightly on the wheel of the SUV they'd bought with money forwarded by Brooks from the company's slush fund.

After Elijah had dropped them off at a car rental place, they'd waited until he'd left and then Gage had changed plans and they'd gone across the street to a used car dealership—where they'd bought the vehicle instead of renting. All cash, all off the books. Exactly the way they did business. He'd used one of his many fake IDs, so if something happened and they had to ditch the vehicle, it wouldn't be traced back to them.

"I really don't like this," he murmured. "She was supposed to meet you there alone and now her fiancé is coming?"

"I don't like it either, but it is what it is. Trust me, as soon as I get her alone, I'll be able to find out what's going on. So I'll meet her for dinner, make pleasant conversation for a while, and then we'll do that whole girl thing and go to the bathroom together. If she's able, she'll tell me what's going on."

"Brooks rented the Presidential Suite for me, so I'll be checking in as well. And no matter what, I'm going to have your back through all of this. After dinner, I'll meet you in your room."

She wasn't sure that was such a good idea. "Are you sure? I'm supposed to be showing up alone."

He snorted softly. "I'm not going to get caught."

"Okay. I know you're a pro. This is just really personal for me. I'm...scared for Layla."

"I would never do anything to get your friend hurt. Ever."

She believed him and, more than that, she trusted him in a way she didn't trust many people. She'd learned the hard way that many were assholes. That loyalties could turn on a dime. Her perspective had shifted slightly since she'd started working with the people of Redemption Harbor Consulting. They were *her* people now.

"So, are we ever going to talk about what happened between us?" she blurted into the growing silence of the SUV, then inwardly winced.

Gage had held her all night, but then this morning when she'd woken up he'd been out of bed and ready to go. Since then it had been back to business as usual. She thought maybe he'd been distant because Elijah was with them. But once they'd bought the used SUV, it had been more of the same. And he'd been mostly quiet on the way to the spa. They'd stopped at a couple places to buy a new laptop and appropriate clothing for her for the spa. And he hadn't been cold, exactly, but he had been standoffish.

"Look, Nova, we're on a job."

"So?"

"I'm your boss."

She snorted softly.

But he continued. "I'm in a position of power over you, and I never want to take advantage. I never want you to feel pressured to do anything."

"Well, technically you might be my boss, but you can't fire me. I have an employment contract and only Skye has the authority to fire me. So yeah, you're a cofounder, but you don't have authority over me."

"It's still not right." His jaw tightened again, and he wouldn't even glance at her.

"That sounds like a whole lot of excuses to me. If you don't want a relationship with me, you just have to say it. You don't have to give me bullshit reasons." She thought they were better friends than that. That he could give it to her straight. Right now, he was giving her garbage.

"It's not bullshit." His tone was neutral enough she knew that even *he* didn't believe the crap coming out of his mouth.

She sniffed once and looked out the window at the passing scenery. Wide open spaces and snowcapped mountains in the distance flew by. She wasn't going to argue with him, even if it was complete and utter bullshit. She was trying to wrap her head around the sudden change in Gage. He'd seemed different after the crash, as if he was ready to try something real with her.

Even though she knew him pretty well, Gage had always been fairly tightlipped about his past. They hung out with each other and joked around a lot, but she had no idea about his previous relationships. She wondered if that might have something to do with this wall he was putting up. Or maybe he simply didn't want anything more with her.

"You're physically attracted to me," she said, because she simply couldn't help herself. That had never been her strong suit—keeping her opinions to herself.

"I'm more attracted to you than I've ever been attracted to anyone. Ever." His words were practically a growl.

She blinked at the intensity in his voice. The words were said with such conviction that she believed him. So…he was physically attracted to her and the chemistry between them was insane—and mutual. What the hell was wrong, then? The boss excuse was weak. There had to be more to it.

She wanted to push him, but held back for now. Because he was right about one thing. They were on a job, and Layla's safety was the number one issue right now. Nova didn't want to muddle everything up with emotions and drama. Not when Layla's life was on the line. But soon enough, she was going to get some answers from Gage.

* * *

Nova glanced around the hotel room as the door shut behind her. It was plush, inviting, and made it clear that Layla's fiancé had money. According to her friend, he'd insisted on paying for Nova's room too.

Not the Presidential Suite, like Gage's, but it was on one of the higher floors and right across the hall from Layla's room.

Nova knew that Gage would be checking the room for bugs while she was at dinner, but it still felt weird knowing this place might be rigged with cameras or listening devices.

It seemed unlikely, but considering her current field of work and her previous one with the CIA, nothing actually surprised her anymore. And since they didn't know what they were up against with this guy, she reminded herself that yes, anything was possible.

So she just went about her business, acting as if everything was normal. She pulled out her clothes for the night: an off-the-shoulder gray sweater, formfitting black pants, ankle boots with low heels and little skulls on the side—which Gage had picked out when they'd gone shopping—and a small black clutch that also had little skulls and crossbones covering it. For her jewelry, she'd chosen big everything: silver hoops, jangly bracelets and a silver Y-necklace. Again, Gage had picked them too, surprising her. Of all people, she knew how much appearances could matter, so for tonight, she was going for the trendy, carefree friend of Layla's. Not the former CIA analyst who now worked for a company that took on gray-area jobs.

Leaving everything on the bed, she made her way to the shower, glad the pain in her knee was easing. She felt as if she was on autopilot getting ready. Knowing Gage was out there and had her back eased some of the tension, but considering what was lingering between them, not much.

She was annoyed at him and, okay, at herself. But mainly she was pissed at him for acting like he knew best, like if they denied what was between them it would simply go away. What the hell did he think, that if they just pretended all that raw heat wasn't real they could go back to being friends?

She certainly wasn't going to chase after him, however. If he wanted to keep things strictly professional, they would. But she wasn't so sure she was going to sit around waiting for him anymore. She'd turned down a helluva lot of dates since moving to Redemption Harbor, and for no discernible reason.

Well, there was a reason. A tall, frustratingly sexy one who was seriously messing with her head right now.

But she had to stop putting her life on hold, hoping he would notice her. Because he *had* noticed her—and he didn't want a relationship.

She mentally shook herself and stepped into the huge shower. She had to forget about all of this right now and keep her head on straight. Soon she'd be meeting with

Layla's fiancé and hopefully finding out what the hell was going on with her friend.

And then she planned to get Layla out of here.

CHAPTER TEN

—Don't die with regrets.—

From the bar inside the restaurant of the exclusive spa they were staying at, Gage covertly watched as Nova sat at a table with her friend Layla and the woman's fiancé. A man he had a growing and interesting file on. Gage had simply wanted to get eyes on Nova before he headed up to her room to do a scan. He'd already hacked into the security system of the resort and, to give them credit, they clearly valued their clients' privacy. There wasn't an obscene amount of video cameras, which might be a hindrance to him later. He wanted eyes everywhere, but they didn't have cameras in some sections of the resort.

He'd make it work. He always did.

Gage slightly straightened as a man approached Nova's table. Brody Kingston clearly knew the man, if his smile was any indication. Standing, he shook the man's hand and invited him to join them.

Gage had already told the bartender to charge his room—which was under an alias, of course—so he stood and adjusted the volume on his earpiece. Even if he wanted to stay and see how this played out, he needed to scan Nova's room. But he would be listening.

114 | KATIE REUS

There was nothing inherently wrong with the way the newcomer looked at Nova, but it was clear he was interested in her. And who could blame him? She was perfect. Gage gritted his teeth, but used the mirror above the bar to watch them covertly.

It was time for him to get out of here. He was on a job, and he couldn't act like some jealous boyfriend. Hell, when Colt and Skye worked together, Colt was always professional when it came to his wife. Gage seriously didn't understand how the man could be so damn evolved when it came to her. Skye was going to be the best woman in another man's wedding and Colt was fine with it—was fine with her friendship with Axel. The two of them acted like children when they were together. It was funny, but Gage wasn't so certain he'd be okay with Nova having such a close relationship with someone of the opposite sex. And that made him feel pretty shitty inside.

Shaking those thoughts away, he left. He had to get the hell out of here.

"Richard, you of course know Layla." Kingston's voice came through his earpiece loud and clear. The listening device they'd sewn into the lining of Nova's purse was perfect. "This is her dear friend, Nova."

Nova murmured a polite but disinterested response.

"It's a surprise to see you, but a welcome one," Richard said.

As soon as Gage was able, he'd grab Richard's image from the security feed he'd hacked earlier and run it through a facial recognition program. It seemed odd that a single man would be at a spa by himself. Or maybe Gage simply wasn't as metrosexual as the dude.

"You're here alone?" There was a hint of amusement in Nova's voice as she asked the man what Gage had been thinking.

Gage snorted to himself as he stepped onto the elevator.

The man laughed lightly. "I've got business in Billings and decided to stay here because of the atmosphere."

There were more polite murmurings and Kingston ordered a bottle of wine, but Gage was able to tune most of it out as he reached Nova's floor.

Gage waited until it was clear of people before using the key card he'd created as a master card to infiltrate any room. And he'd already messed with the security camera on this floor so that it was on a loop for the next hour. It shouldn't take him long to scan her bedroom.

Once inside, he got to work, moving efficiently and methodically. He'd done scans like this many times before and had a system. There were always obvious places to hide bugs and then not so obvious ones. As a hacker, he knew them all. Using a wand, he scanned for any type of electronic interference.

As Gage finished his recon of the hotel room, he froze at the sound of a door handle rattling. He could hear Nova still talking through his earpiece and it was way too soon for her to be done with dinner so he reacted quickly, racing across the room and ducking out onto the balcony.

He shut the door behind him, leaving it cracked open ever so slightly. The drapes were mostly drawn with only a few inches visible but he saw two men step into the room through the opening. So he moved back farther into the shadows.

The men didn't speak to each other as they started sweeping the room. It didn't look as if they were planting anything, and they weren't wearing gloves. No, they were simply riffling through her suitcase and drawers.

When one of them took a step toward the balcony doors, Gage tensed, debating his options. He could take two guys on if he had to. Or he might be able to make his way to another balcony—jump down to the next one or climb to the neighboring one.

But that was dangerous, especially at night and without backup. Not to mention a guest might see him, report it and then that could get Nova attention she didn't need. But if he revealed himself, it would blow Nova's cover and they couldn't risk that. Not now. *Shit.*

"What the hell are you doing? She doesn't have anything hidden on the balcony, stupid." There was annoyance in the other man's tone.

The man with his fingers on the balcony door turned then shot the guy the finger. "Just being thorough. Not sure why we're even searching her room anyway."

"Because the boss wants us to. He just wants to make sure his woman's friend isn't some narc."

"Did you see the body on her? No way she's a fucking narc. That woman is prime rib."

"And you wonder why you're single?" the other guy muttered as he opened another drawer.

"I'm just saying, she's hoooot." Dragging out the word "hot," groaning as he said it, the man looked under the bed once before popping back up. Then he moved to the nightstand.

"Who cares if she's hot? A woman who looks that good? She's going to be high-maintenance. No thanks."

"Layla's not high-maintenance and she's smokin' too."

"Shut the fuck up with that right now." The guy with dark hair and a mustache—the one with the brain—stilled and stared at his friend. "You don't talk about her. Ever. He's marrying her. You gotta respect that."

The other guy shrugged as he opened the closet doors. "I'm not disrespecting her. I like her. But I was just saying, she was a schoolteacher. Of course she's not high-maintenance. I think it's like an unwritten rule. She's gotta be grateful for how much the boss gives her. He treats her right."

Tense, Gage remained where he was as the two men continued talking—and not quietly either. When the subject shifted to some sports game, some of the tension inside him eased. He didn't like hearing two strangers talking about Nova in any capacity and the clock was ticking down before he needed to get the hell out of here. That video loop he'd added only lasted so long. And if he missed that time frame and Kingston decided to get curious and saw him exiting Nova's room?

Nope. He couldn't let that happen.

Though it only took them ten minutes to look through her stuff, it seemed like forever—and he hated that they'd touched her things at all. It felt like a violation. Once they left, he waited another solid five minutes, wanting to make sure they were truly gone before he finished what he needed to do. He ran a quick scan with his wand over all the stuff they'd touched.

Once he was completely satisfied that the room was secure, only then did he let himself out—and ignore the silky black thong tossed onto the floor next to some of her clothes. Nova was a little messy, which seemed at odds with her organized personality.

Not that he cared one way or the other, but the thought of her wearing those? Of him tugging them down her legs with his teeth… He rolled his shoulders once as he stepped out into the hallway. All clear.

He could hear that the dinner was winding down, so instead of heading back to the bar, he went straight to the Presidential Suite. He checked his own security feeds that he'd set up, and even though no one showed up on his camera, he did a quick, basic scan of the room for his own peace of mind.

He'd left strict instructions with the resort that he wasn't to be bothered while he was here. They hadn't seemed surprised by his request either, so he knew it wasn't out of the ordinary.

Pulling up the security feeds he'd hacked into, he zeroed in on Nova so he could see her as well as listen in while she talked and laughed with her friend.

Her body language made it clear she had no interest in Richard whatever-his-last-name-was. She smiled politely when he poured another glass of wine for her, but didn't make a move to touch it.

"I need to use the ladies' room," Layla said after laughing at something her fiancé said. "Join me?" she asked Nova, her smile firmly in place.

As the women stood, Gage froze an image of the newcomer's face and plugged it into one of his facial recognition programs. If he didn't get a hit with this one, he had others he could tap into. It was pretty rare that someone could hide from him. And if he decided to hunt someone...he always got his prey.

* * *

Nova kept her smile firmly in place as she stood, even though the last half hour had felt awkward. The conversation had been pleasant enough—and boring as grass growing. Which was what made it all awkward. Normally she and Layla would be talking about their lives and making inappropriate comments about, well, whatever. Anything and everything.

Layla's fiancé was definitely charming, but Nova didn't buy any of it. And she wasn't certain she would have bought the charming act even if she hadn't known something was wrong. Something about him bothered her, but she couldn't define what it was. He wasn't creepy toward her and hadn't given her any once-overs. He was handsome, charming and he was definitely into Layla, but…who knew? Layla wasn't herself around the man. She was a muted version of herself. All quiet and reserved. Not the Layla Ferrer that Nova had grown up with—the girl who'd taken a baseball bat to a guy who tried to hurt Layla.

"Somehow we'll manage without you two," the man sitting next to her said.

Even if she wanted to roll her eyes, she smiled back and responded with something boring and appropriate as she grabbed her small clutch. She thought about leaving it in case the two men said something interesting so Gage could get it recorded. But if for some reason Kingston was suspicious of her and decided to check her purse…No, couldn't risk it. It would put Layla in danger.

Once they were in the bathroom, Layla held a finger to her lips. Her chestnut brown hair was pulled into a knot at the back of her neck, showing off huge diamond earrings—definitely real and no doubt a gift from Kingston. The sweater dress she wore hugged all her curves, but Nova had known her a long time, and Layla had lost weight. If she had to guess, it wasn't intentional. Nova nodded and waited as Layla checked the three stalls. Then they waited a few more minutes until the single woman inside one of them left.

"It's so good to see you," Layla said once they were alone, her unique amber-colored eyes filled with worry. "I hope you don't mind my fiancé tagging along tonight."

"Of course not," Nova said, even as Layla pulled out a small little notepad with butterflies on the paper. She started writing furiously, so Nova continued talking about benign things. "This place is gorgeous. You couldn't have picked a better location for a girls' getaway."

"I figured it was something you would like, though I'm sorry about your knee."

"It's okay," Nova said. "I'm just a little sore and moving slower than normal, but I figure all this therapy will help." She let out a laugh that sounded a little airheaded but she didn't care.

Layla gave the note to her and then turned on one of the sinks.

Nova read quickly.

I don't think he's bugged me, but I simply don't know. He surprised me at the last minute and decided to join me. And I couldn't tell him no. I saw him murder a DEA agent inside his pool house. I wasn't supposed to be home that day. And I don't know who to trust because there was another agent with Brody at the time. He had on a badge and weapon and I'd met him before, so I know who he is. Feel like my whole world is crumbling. I know who you used to work for. I'm sorry I brought you into this. But I need to tell someone. I need help getting away from him. No idea what he'll do if he finds out what I saw.

Nova simply took the pen from Layla as Layla talked about what color polish she was going to get tomorrow for their pedicure.

She wrote quickly. *I'm not alone. Backup with me. He's hacked into the entire security system. The plan is to leave tomorrow during one of our spa sessions. We'll leave here then figure out what to do. Have contacts you can talk to. We'll keep you safe.*

After she handed it to Layla and her friend had a chance to read it, tears filled her eyes as she simply nodded and mouthed "Thank you."

Then Layla took the paper and put it in the sink. The water washed over it, dissolving all the ink, and eventually the paper itself crumbled, the pieces sliding down the drain.

Nova pulled her best friend into a hug and squeezed tight. She wanted to tell Layla that everything would be okay, that she was going to be safe soon. So she injected all of that into her hug. Because it was true.

She wouldn't rest until Layla was far away from here. After what Layla had just told her? This was a whole new ballgame. Not exactly what Nova had been expecting. There would be things to decide, like what would happen if she testified against the man. Would she go into WITSEC? Or would she simply want to disappear and start over somewhere fresh? Nova had a lot of questions, but now was not the time.

Nova wasn't sure how she got through the rest of dinner smiling her fake smiles and pretending everything was okay, all the while knowing that her best friend had to return to her own suite with her murderous fiancé, Brody Kingston. She wasn't sure how Layla was holding up.

Of all people, Nova understood living in gray areas. She'd done it with the CIA and she now did it for Redemption Harbor Consulting. But at the end of the day, she could look at herself in the mirror. The people her company targeted were bad guys, to put it in simple terms. And the people they helped had nowhere else to turn.

Killing a federal agent? No wonder Layla was scared. At least they would be able to put her in contact with the right people. Most likely Leighton's FBI friend, Hazel. She might not be a totally straight arrow—she wouldn't be working with them if she was—but she was trustworthy and she got the job done. More importantly, she would protect Layla and get her in touch with the right people. Likely the marshals. If that was what Layla wanted to do. Nova couldn't imagine Layla not wanting to testify. She wouldn't want to simply go on the run and hide the rest of her life. But if she did, Nova would support her no matter what.

Sliding the key card into her suite's door, she breathed a sigh of relief as she slipped out of her small-heeled boots. Gage had texted her that her room was clean, so she felt free to be herself. She was still going to act as if she was being observed—better safe than sorry—but it felt good to have that sort of freedom now.

She'd barely taken one step into the big suite when an arm snaked around her waist from behind.

She went into fight mode and started to elbow her would-be attacker when she smelled Gage—just as he murmured, "It's me."

Nova turned in his arms, ready to ream him out for scaring the crap out of her, when he backed her up against the nearest wall and crushed his mouth over hers.

Say what?

She should push him off but instead she arched into him, her covered breasts rubbing against his chest as heat pooled between her legs. This man got her revved up and ready to go, from zero to sixty just like that. Damn it, what the hell was wrong with her?

Nova moaned into his mouth as he shoved his fingers through her hair. She'd pulled it back with a couple sparkly clips, but he released them, letting her hair tumble free around her shoulders as he completely dominated her.

He rolled his hips against her, his erection hard as stone as he ate at her mouth like a man starving.

She wanted to ask him what about his stupid rules on not dating her, not getting involved, but it was hard to think of *anything* as he plundered her mouth with his tongue and cupped the back of her head.

When he slid one of his big hands down to her hip and clutched her oh so possessively, she didn't think, just reacted. She hoisted up and wrapped her legs around him. Her knee twinged in discomfort and this was moving way too fast, but she didn't care. She'd been fantasizing about this, about *him*, since practically the moment they'd met. Hell, from that first ridiculous phone conversation when he'd been a total dick. She'd loved the sound of his voice even as he'd been rude. Of course, she'd hung up on him. Then when they'd met in person? Oooh yeah.

He kept her pinned against the wall as he practically devoured her. Her nipples beaded tightly against her bra, and with each movement the friction as she arched into him turned her on even more.

As he pulled away from her mouth, she started to protest until he nibbled along her jawline with sharp little bites.

"Didn't like the way that guy was looking at you," he growled.

"You're jealous?" Seriously? How was that even possible?

"Yeah." Another soft nip of her skin.

She wanted to be flattered and, okay, she was, but... She pressed a hand against his chest and he stopped, breathing hard as he pulled back to look at her.

She was still pinned against the wall, her legs wrapped tightly around him, his cock firmly against her spread thighs. "Is that...why you're here? You got jealous?"

He didn't deny it, just watched her carefully.

Her lust started to fade. "So if a random guy hadn't shown up at dinner, you wouldn't be here?"

He didn't respond. Which was answer enough.

She shoved against his chest and let her legs fall. Her knee ached but she ignored it as hurt spread through her. "You can't screw with my head, Gage. If you want to be friends, fine, but I'm not a yo-yo. You can't jerk me around because…whatever. The reason doesn't even matter. This is garbage, and I'm not doing it. Especially not now."

He shoved a hand through his hair, the action agitated and jerky. "The last thing I want to do is mess with you. I'm all twisted up right now, Nova. I can't think straight around you."

"Well, you're going to need to. We have to be perfect tomorrow." Because no matter what, they were getting Layla out of there tomorrow. "So go back to your room and do whatever it is you need to do. I need to get some sleep."

Gage nodded slowly, taking a step back from her. Damn him, he looked sexy in his slightly rumpled shirt.

Nope. No, no, no.

Gritting her teeth, she turned away from him, not even wanting to look at him right now. She couldn't believe him with this jealousy bullshit. He knew she wanted him, wanted…a relationship with him. *Ugh.*

Once Layla was safe and life went back to normal—or normalish—she was getting over Gage. Tonight had just driven home the point that she needed to. He'd come to her room to satisfy some stupid caveman urge. He didn't have a claim on her—and he never would. And she couldn't put up with him yanking her around like her feelings didn't matter.

CHAPTER ELEVEN

—Be brave.—

"Your friend Nova is charming." Brody's voice was light as he stripped off his jacket and laid it on the back of the tufted chair next to the king-size bed.

"She's great." Layla didn't turn around to face him as she slid off her heels. Too many emotions ran rampant through her right now. Relief and fear warred inside, both clawing for dominance. All while she tried to keep her cool. She was engaged to a monster.

"Richard definitely thought so," he continued.

Before she could stop herself, Layla snorted and started taking off her earrings—a gift from Brody that she'd once loved. She glanced at him in the mirror.

"What?" he asked.

"Richard is the most boring man on the planet. Definitely not Nova's type."

Brody smiled then, back to Mr. Charming. Under normal circumstances, that smile would have melted her. Not anymore.

Not ever again.

"I'm sorry he interrupted our dinner."

She simply nodded and tried to smile, but it was hard. His friend hadn't interrupted, Brody had invited him.

"You're annoyed with me," Brody said suddenly.

She knew she needed to play things right but she wasn't going to hide her annoyance. Because she didn't think he'd buy it. She might have let him take the lead in so many things previously, but she hadn't been a complete pushover during their relationship. She couldn't let this slide.

After she took her second earring out and set it on the countertop, she turned to face him. "Yes, I am. I came here for a girls' weekend with my best friend. A friend I haven't seen in over a year. And then you show up, which is fine, but *then* you invite some random guy to have dinner with us. I wanted to spend the evening catching up with my best friend. A woman who is like a sister to me." She crossed her arms over her chest, anger and fear surging through her.

For the first time since she'd known him, Brody's façade started to crack. Little fissures that showed a glimpse of the monster beneath the mask. God, how had she not seen this before? He was actually angry at her. *At her.* When she'd done nothing wrong.

"I'm sorry," he murmured, stepping closer as he placed his hands on her hips. "It was thoughtless of me. Of course you want to spend time with your best friend. Tomorrow you have a whole spa day set up, right?"

She nodded tightly, fighting not to cringe away from his touch. "Yes."

"I'll stay out of your hair tomorrow. I promise," he murmured. "And I'll make it up to you right now." Leaning down, he nuzzled her neck, gently nipping at her earlobe.

Once upon a time, that would have softened her up and turned her on. Not that they argued much. Because she usually just let him have his way. Something she was only now realizing. God, she felt like a fool.

His touch made her shiver, and not in a good way. She was so close to escaping. Her best friend had backup. They could leave tomorrow. *Tomorrow*. So if that meant that she had to have sex with Brody right now, she'd grit her teeth and do it. She'd even pretend she wanted it.

Forcing herself to relax, she slid her hands up his chest and over his shoulders.

When his phone buzzed in his pocket, he let out an annoyed curse and pulled back.

"I have some business to take care of," he murmured, frowning at the screen. "I have to go out. I'm not sure how long I'll be."

She wanted to do a fist pump, but simply nodded in understanding. "That's okay. If you'll be gone, I'll probably head across the hall and spend time with Nova. I might just stay over there tonight, since we didn't get any time together." She threw that last barb in because she couldn't help herself.

It was clear that he definitely didn't like that, but he didn't push back. "I've got my phone on me if you need anything. And I'll have someone watching out for you two. Gotta keep my girl safe." He brushed his lips over hers before quietly leaving the room.

Layla ran a shaking hand through her hair. So close. She was so damn close.

Picking up her own phone, she texted Nova. *I'll be over in just a few minutes if that's okay? How about we order desserts from room service and watch a movie?*

It took longer than she'd expected for Nova to respond, a full two minutes. When it came, however, relief won out over her fear.

Yes! I'm already in my PJs. Let's get chocolate and wine.

Perfect. God, just a few more hours and she'd be free. Maybe they could even leave tonight. Probably not, since Brody had guys watching her room. Supposedly, anyway. Not that she doubted him. And he'd seemed a little off tonight, too, so she didn't want to push her luck.

Tomorrow though, this would be over. She wasn't sure what the future held, but she had to get the hell away from her fiancé.

* * *

As Layla stepped into her room, pajamas on and her expression tight, Nova quickly scribbled on a pad of paper that the room wasn't bugged. But Layla was clearly nervous and edgy.

Leaving tomorrow. We have a plan, Nova wrote.

Brody is gone tonight. He said he's got some men keeping an eye out for me but maybe we could try tonight?

How many guys?

Two normally but he sometimes puts three on me. I don't think they're right in the hallway. Maybe we could try? Panic was raw and real in her best friend's eyes.

Nova picked up her phone and texted Gage. *Can we try leaving tonight? Maybe you can use the video system to watch out for Kingston's guys.*

She received a text two excruciatingly long minutes later. *Head up to my room.* Then he texted her the code to input.

She nodded once at Layla.

The relief that bled into her gaze punched through Nova. She quickly packed her bag and then shoved it under the bed. She couldn't take it, otherwise it would be obvious they were leaving. They would just have to figure something out later, not that she really cared about a bunch of clothes.

Kingston knew who she was anyway and he knew where she lived—or he could find out easily enough. Good thing they wouldn't be going back to her home. Nope, they had a much more secure location in mind.

"Let's head down to the bar and grab another bottle of champagne. I don't feel like waiting on room service to deliver something to us," Nova said casually so Layla would understand what their cover would be in case they ran into any of Kingston's men.

Layla nodded in understanding and slipped on her shoes at the door.

Their night clothes were more like casual lounge clothes so they looked normal enough stepping out into the hallway.

All clear, she mouthed to Layla.

Keeping their movements casual, they headed down the hallway toward the huge set of elevators.

Nova was glad they were getting out of here tonight as opposed to tomorrow. Even though it wasn't that much longer, it felt like an eternity and each second they were in the same vicinity as Layla's fiancé was one second too long. She just wanted to get her the hell out of here.

Her phone buzzed right as the elevator doors opened. Next to her Layla slightly stiffened so Nova didn't check her text. She didn't have to. She recognized one of Kingston's men on the elevator—no doubt a message from Gage. Damn it, she should have just put the earpiece back in, but she wasn't used to wearing them.

"What are you doing?" The man in the elevator asked Layla, completely ignoring Nova.

Though she couldn't show it, she recognized him from one of the files Gage had created.

"Headed down to the bar to get champagne," Layla said smoothly, smiling neutrally at one of Kingston's men.

His frown deepened. "Why not just call room service?"

Nova took over then, linking her arm through Layla's. Then she spoke just a little too loudly, acting as if she was tipsy. "We don't feel like waiting for room service. And it's really none of your business what we're doing," she said tartly.

The man simply sighed and half rolled his eyes. Layla gave an exasperated smile in Nova's direction.

Nova's heart was racing as they pressed the down button instead of heading for the Presidential suite. Now they would actually have to go through with what they'd said and there was no way they could risk leaving tonight.

Just in case Kingston's man was on to them, which Nova doubted. But he would be paying attention now that she and Layla had deviated from what they'd said they would be doing.

She needed to text Gage, but he was no doubt seeing all this from his master vantage point via the computers.

She just hoped Layla was able to maintain her façade and hang on a little bit longer.

CHAPTER TWELVE

—Life is not a fairy tale. If you lose your shoe at
midnight, you're drunk.—

"How can you just *not* know who she worked for
before?" Brody demanded, far too annoyed before he'd even finished his lunch. Layla hadn't come back
to the room last night—of course, he hadn't been back
until two in the morning anyway. But he'd been hoping
for time with her. And he wanted more information on
her friend, Nova. He should have had the woman looked
into earlier, but he'd had a lot to deal with lately. And
this trip had been last minute. At least his guys hadn't
found anything important in her room. Just clothes and
women's stuff.

His business associate, Richard—aka Ricardo Diaz—
lifted a shoulder and took a sip of his coffee. "It's just
what I said. Her first job out of college was for a tech
company, but I've been doing this long enough that I'm
ninety percent sure she worked for the government. The
company is set up a certain way, and if I had to guess, I'd
say CIA. I have no idea in what capacity she worked for
them, however. After college, her online presence basically vanished. And she has no social media."

That alone bothered Brody. Almost everyone had social media. Even Layla did, though hers was limited and she only used it to keep in touch with the women she used to work with.

So for Nova not to have anything? It could mean nothing, but his gut was telling him otherwise. Layla had been friends with Nova for over a decade. She'd told him how they'd spent time together in foster care and how she'd basically lived with Nova's family. Though it hadn't sounded like much of a family.

Not like he had any room to judge, considering he'd basically grown up like a wild animal.

He tapped his finger against the table where he sat in Richard's suite.

It wasn't as if the only reason he'd come here was to keep an eye on his fiancée—though she had been acting a little off the past couple weeks. At first he'd thought she might be pregnant, but that wasn't the case. And she'd been pushing back more against him. It had been subtle, but it agitated him. He'd thought their roles were clearly defined in their relationship. She'd even agreed to stop teaching. She said it was only for a year. But he didn't plan to let her return to work at all. He'd simply get her pregnant and then she wouldn't want to return to work.

Because he wanted her at home where she belonged. Where she could raise the kids they would have. She was educated, beautiful, and she didn't question him about his business. She was the perfect woman for him, and she would never cheat. No, Layla was loyal, and she deserved the same from him.

Mentally shaking himself, he shoved thoughts of her friend away for the moment. He would worry about that puzzle later. He simply liked knowing everything about everybody in his life. Since Nova was going to be in their wedding, he was just being cautious.

"I'll worry about her later. How are things looking on your end?" he asked, wanting to focus on more important topics.

Richard adjusted his blue Christian Lacroix tie. "All the product is ready to go."

"Supply line is good on my end. My guys have done some test runs and had no issues." Nothing they couldn't handle anyway. Brody worked with various individuals: a biker gang, independent contractors, and of course he had some federal agents in his pocket. All to make sure the supply line of drugs he oversaw made it across the border into Canada. He got his product from the Romero cartel and, though his main operation was in Chicago, he ran a lot of drugs across the Montana border. Mainly heroin, fentanyl and lately, carfentanil—which was normally manufactured in Asia, but recently his Mexican contacts had been pushing it hard. And he was very careful to keep himself insulated. Though occasionally he had to get his hands dirty.

They spoke for another ten minutes, ironing out details until finally, they were done. He liked Richard well enough, but he never forgot the two of them weren't friends. They were simply business associates. Richard's loyalty was to the cartel. Always would be.

Standing, he said, "I'll speak to you later. I need to check in with my guys." He'd put two men on Nova and Layla. Because of his profession, he needed Layla watched all the time. For her own safety. She might not have any idea what he did for a living, but others did, and that could make her a target. She belonged to him, so he would take care of her. Unless she crossed him, of course. But he couldn't imagine that ever happening. She was soft and sweet, a fucking teacher, for chrissakes.

His phone buzzed in his pocket so he glanced at the screen. From Lucas, his head of security. *Women still inside doing girly shit.*

He snorted at the text even as his frustration with Layla grew. She had been angry with him about showing up here. Which pissed him off, considering he was the one who'd paid for this. He had a right to do whatever the hell he wanted where she was concerned. They were going to be married.

As he rubbed the back of his neck, he texted back with his free hand that he'd be indisposed for a while. He needed to get a massage. Something had to ease his tension, considering he and Layla hadn't fucked for a week. That was likely why he was so agitated.

When he was done, he'd buy her a new necklace and fix things with her. Jewelry should work in soothing her anger. Even if her recent behavior annoyed him, she was still his, and he would make this right. He'd learned at a young age that beating a significant other was stupid. It was how his own father had ended up dead. When his mother had shoved a six-inch blade right into his back.

The bastard had deserved it too. No, giving Layla gifts would be much smarter. All that sparkle would distract his woman and keep her oblivious to what she was about to marry into.

* * *

"Just put this in your ear," Nova said quietly as they stepped into the pool area of the spa. They'd had manicures, pedicures and facials. In an hour, they were supposedly going to get massages, but they wouldn't be showing up for their appointment. Nope. During this hour of "downtime" by the pool, they would be leaving instead.

"What's this for?" Layla murmured, sliding it into her ear.

Without their cell phones or other people nearby, they were free to talk as they walked along the edge of the indoor pool. Heated, it was covered by a huge glass dome. So they would stay warm and protected from the outdoor weather. "In case anything happens and we get separated, we'll be able to communicate."

"Oh, right."

Gage had let Nova know earlier that there were more than just two of Kingston's guys here. There were at least five that he'd seen on the premises, going in and out of a suite Brody'd been in with the man from last night. Though Gage was fairly certain that only two men were actually keeping an eye out for Layla. But if any one of them saw her leaving the premises, it could arouse suspicion. So they had to stick to their original plan of a spa day, and then leave when the opportunity arose. An opportunity they'd created.

"You okay?"

"Yeah. Nervous." A splash from the nearby pool made Layla jump when a woman dove into the deep end.

Bypassing the pool, they headed toward two cushioned lounge chairs. Nova tightened the belt of the fluffy, spa-provided robe as she sat.

The second they both settled, a woman wearing white pants and a white tunic approached them with a smile and offer of drinks.

They both ordered mimosas and charged it to Layla's room even though Nova had no intention of drinking it. Right now was all about appearances, and she felt no guilt about racking up more charges on Kingston's credit card.

There were five other women in the pool area, one swimming, the others lounging, but they were far enough away they wouldn't be able to overhear anything. Soft classical music pumped through invisible speakers, creating an even more relaxing atmosphere.

"We're almost gone. As soon as we sit for a few minutes, we'll head out," Nova murmured.

"I know. I'm just scared. Terrified, actually. I keep thinking about the future and what's going to happen. At the same time, I simply just want to get out of here. I need to be away from him, free, so I can think clearly."

Nova reached out and squeezed Layla's hand once. "No matter what happens, you're going to be safe." She stopped talking and let her hand drop as the woman from before approached with a smile and two flute-shaped glasses.

They made small talk for a few seconds until the woman left.

"All right, ladies, the distraction is in place," Gage said via their earpieces. "It's time to go."

Next to her, Layla jumped slightly and then gave a half-smile. "I forgot he was on the other end."

"What kind of distraction are we talking here?" Nova asked as she stood with Layla.

Gage snorted softly. "A woman with big breasts to distract one of the security guys."

Despite the situation, Nova let out a laugh. "Sounds like a perfect distraction. How do you know it will work?"

"I gave her five hundred bucks. And told her five hundred more was in it for her if she kept the guy talking for ten minutes and kept his eyes on her breasts. A grand for ten minutes of doing nothing is hard to pass up."

"That should work."

Next to her, Layla downed her flute and rolled her shoulders once. "I'm ready."

Nova kept her steps casual even as energy pumped through her. "I need to get something out of my locker," she said to Layla as they passed an employee. It was seriously unlikely that Kingston had paid anyone to eavesdrop on or watch Layla, but they were playing their roles right now.

This was the reason she never could have been a spy. Not like Skye and Colt had been. Taking on different personas, pretending to be someone she wasn't all the time? No way. It would get far too exhausting, and she simply didn't have the personality for it.

Not too long ago she'd thought she might want to do more operations with the crew, but this was stressing her out. Though that could have more to do with the fact that Layla's life was on the line and not a stranger's.

In the luxurious locker room, they both hung up their robes and wordlessly slid on their clothes—jeans, boots, and sweaters. And a hooded jacket for Layla. If they needed anything else, they'd get it later. Right now was about escaping unnoticed.

If for some reason Layla's fiancé tried to send a message to her through one of the women working today, their glasses were still on the table out there and it would appear as if they'd just stepped away. Cell phones weren't allowed in any of the spa areas except the actual locker room. And that was where Layla was leaving hers.

She was leaving literally everything behind. She'd brought a change of clothes and her wallet, and that was it.

Nova shook her head when Layla started to take off her engagement ring to leave it in the locker with her phone.

"Why not?" she whispered.

"Sell it later. I know you don't want anything of his but if you have to start over...just keep it. Trust me. Those earrings too." She nodded at the diamond earrings. Nova had no doubt the crew would dig into the secret slush fund to help Layla if she needed it, but Nova understood the need to have something of your own, to be able to take care of yourself. Without knowing what kind of savings Layla had or anything she might be able to salvage after this, that ring and the expensive earrings represented a small bit of independence.

"You're right." Layla slid it back in place before tugging gloves on. It was in the low forties today so they needed to layer.

Nova twisted her long hair into a tight bun at her nape, then slid her own thick, cotton mittens on. "We're ready," she said quietly.

"Just another minute." Gage's voice was quiet, intense, then... "Okay, you guys are clear. Exit out of the southwest door into the parking lot. One of Kingston's guys is currently talking to his distraction. You should be good. I don't see anyone else stationed in this parking lot, and I've been scanning the camera feeds. Be careful anyway."

"Layla has a hood on her jacket. It should help," Nova said even as she pushed the exit door open. It wasn't an emergency exit but she was fairly certain it would lock behind them. Didn't matter, they weren't coming back.

Gage had cleaned out her room earlier so she had nothing left behind. The only bad thing was that Kingston knew who Nova was and where she lived. They wouldn't be going back to her place anytime soon though, and the Feds should be able to do their job once Layla talked to them and told them what she'd witnessed.

"I see you both," Gage said. "Keep heading south through that line of parked cars. I'm in the white utility van next to the black two-door Mercedes."

Nova saw the lights flash once and could see a small trail of white smoke from the exhaust. So did Layla, if her slight intake of breath was any indication. Her best friend was quiet as they moved quickly through the parked cars. They couldn't run or draw attention to themselves. No one was back here anyway. No one except one of Kingston's guys. He'd have to be to the west of them near the building, but she wasn't going to turn and look. Gage had told her earlier that he'd been leaning against one of the walls, looking as bored as anything as he kept an eye on this side of the building. So an attractive woman was a good distraction.

As they reached the van, Nova let the relief course through her. But it was short-lived.

"Layla?" a male voice called out.

"Don't—"

Before she'd gotten the sentence out, Layla turned around.

Damn it. Whoever the guy was might not have realized it was Layla if she hadn't reacted to the sound of her name.

"Get in," Nova muttered as she practically shoved Layla through the open door of the van.

Layla cursed and jumped in.

"Another guy was in a parked SUV. I didn't pick him up on my scans," Gage muttered as he kicked the vehicle into drive.

"That was probably John," Layla said, her voice shaking. "Lucas is the one racing toward him."

Through the van window, Nova saw a man wearing a pullover sweater, thick jacket and jeans—Lucas Jimenez, according to Gage—racing over to a parked SUV. Dark-haired Jimenez was on his phone as he reached the vehicle.

When Gage turned in the parking lot, she lost sight of the men. Which meant nothing. They still might catch up.

"We're going to ditch this van then head to the private airport. But we've gotta be sure we lose them first," Gage muttered, more to himself than them.

"I'm so sorry," Layla said, still turned around and looking out the back of the van.

"No need to be sorry," Nova said. "We've got a pilot on standby." She shuddered at the thought of getting inside any sort of flying contraption at this point, but she would do anything for Layla. "There's a helicopter that's going to take us to another rendezvous point."

"Okay," her friend said as she wrapped her arms around herself. "He's going to come after me—"

"One step at a time. We're getting out of here now and then heading to a safe house. From there, we'll figure out what to do."

"I can never repay you enough for—"

"Just stop right there. I know you would do anything for me. I don't ever need thanks."

Layla nodded, though she didn't seem convinced. Her eyes were wide and she had the look of someone close to going into shock. She was a teacher, for God's sake. She never should have been dragged into this. Nova wanted to kick Kingston's ass for that alone. Well, that and a lot of stuff.

* * *

Gage watched the rearview mirror before he took a hard left out of the resort's parking lot.

The SUV was gaining speed as it tore after them. No matter what, it was going to be damn impossible to lose the vehicle. They weren't in a big city, but on the out-skirts in no-man's-land. Even if for some reason he did lose the two men, they might figure out where he was going with the women. So instead of heading toward the airport, he took a right, in the opposite direction.

"What are you doing?" Nova asked quietly. A quick glance at her in the rearview mirror told him she had her own weapon out and down by her side. Well, it was his SIG, but she'd commandeered it for now.

"I've got to stop them before we find a new vehicle. And I need to lead them away from the airport."

She nodded.

Stretched out in front of them were what would have been full green yards during the summer, but now they were brown, dry landscape. Homes dotted this two-lane stretch of highway, a good mile in between each property.

Instead of speeding up when he saw the SUV following them, he started to slow. There was simply no way to outrun these guys here. Not without getting someone killed. He didn't care about his pursuers, but he did care about Nova and Layla.

"They're gaining on us!" Layla cried in panic.

"It's okay. Gage knows what he's doing." The conviction in Nova's voice pleased him.

He'd think about that later, however.

A red four-door sedan flew at them from the other direction before it whooshed past them. No more vehicles as far as he could see. That could change in a minute but for now, this was exactly what he needed.

The other vehicle was getting closer. Closer. Closer.

He couldn't let them get close enough to ram him but he needed them close enough to do what he planned.

"Hold on tight," he ordered, and slammed on the brakes. As the van shuddered to a halt, he jerked it into Park. "If anything happens to me, get her out of here," he snapped at Nova as he jumped from the vehicle, weapon drawn. He trusted her to do what needed to be done.

What he planned was a bold move that could backfire but he trusted his skill, training and experience. For now, it was just two men against him. He could handle this.

The vehicle was about thirty yards away and closing. The driver started to press on the brakes when he saw Gage.

It was far too late.

With his feet spread slightly apart, he aimed and fired. *Pop. Pop. Pop. Pop. Pop.*

The two front tires blew. The car swerved off the road, ramming through a wooden and wire fence.

The barbed wire scraped against the metal of the car with a metallic screech. Job done, he raced back to the van. These guys wouldn't be following. And if they'd called for backup, Gage needed to get the hell out of here before it arrived.

Glass shattered the back window as he slammed his foot down on the gas.

Layla screamed, but Nova turned around and started shooting. The gunfire was over-pronounced in the interior, but he didn't care.

"They ducked back behind the car." Nova's voice was frustrated as he created distance fast.

Wind whistled through the vehicle the faster he drove, but they'd managed to disable their pursuers and had bought some time.

"That was crazy." Nova shook her head as she settled back against the seat. She raised her voice over the wind. "I can't believe you did that."

Bitter cold filled the interior, and the van's heater couldn't combat it. "It was a calculated risk. I liked my odds."

He noticed Layla trembling slightly but she didn't say anything, just leaned into Nova. Nova wrapped her arm around her friend's shoulders and hugged her tight.

"Gotta ditch this vehicle soon. About two miles down the road there's a turnoff, and after that it will be another mile to a local shopping center. Grocery store. We'll steal a car and then head to the airport."

"How do you know all that?" Layla asked.

He lifted a shoulder. "I researched the area."

She simply nodded, closed her eyes and laid her head on Nova's shoulder.

Gage risked another quick glance in the rearview mirror to find Nova watching him intently. The look in her dark eyes was unreadable.

His heart rate had evened out now that they were on the road again. It was possible that a bystander had seen him shoot out the tires, but they'd been in between houses and there had been no one else on the road. So, unlikely. And he doubted those guys were going to call the cops.

It was also possible they'd managed to take a picture of him, and would run his face, but they wouldn't figure out who he was. He was very good at what he did, and covering his tracks was something he'd been doing for a long time.

Up ahead, he took the next turn and allowed himself a sigh of relief. Nova was safe. Yes, he wanted to save her friend, but he wanted Nova back in Redemption Harbor and under lockdown as soon as possible.

That most primitive part of him wanted to keep her safe. To protect her. Not because he thought she couldn't take care of herself, but simply because he needed her to be okay.

Because she was his.

CHAPTER THIRTEEN

—Trust your instinct. It knows what your head hasn't
figured out yet.—

"Sit tight," Gage murmured as he steered into the
open gate of the private airport. There were hangars for private planes, but also a few for sightseeing
tours. Which was where they were going.

"You see anything interesting?" Nova asked from the
back seat of the older-model Jeep they'd stolen—which
she'd hotwired. Apparently something Layla had taught
her long ago.

Hard not to be impressed by that. He felt a little bad
about stealing from someone, but surviving was a hell of
a lot more important now. Besides, they'd leave it at the
hangar in the same shape.

"Maybe. SUV parked outside the hangar we're passing. Two guys talking to someone. Pilot, maybe." He
only glanced at them out of the corner of his eye, not
wanting to seem too interested.

"I can look and see if I recognize anyone," Layla said
from her spot on the floorboards with Nova.

They were piled on top of each other, which he also
felt bad about. But it was a small price to pay for freedom.
"Stay down."

154 | KATIE REUS

He looked over again without being overt, and saw that the man with the two guys in jackets and jeans was now on his phone. The guy was wearing a thick jacket with the logo of his charter business, so yeah, probably a pilot. Nothing particularly out of the ordinary. Still, everyone was suspect now.

"I'm parking on the side of a sightseeing hangar now. We're out of sight of the other hangars now. I see Burton," he said, raising a hand toward the pilot. Skye had put them in contact with Matthew Burton, a former Air Force pilot turned sightseeing pilot. The guy also helped out during any search and rescues in the area if law enforcement needed him. Gage swore that between Skye and Colt, they had contacts—or assets—everywhere. Which was definitely a benefit. "If anyone but me comes up to the Jeep, start shooting."

Nova simply snorted and Layla stared at him as if he'd grown two heads.

"You're sure we can trust the pilot?" Layla asked, her voice trembling.

"One of my partners trusts him, so I trust him."

"Yes," Nova said, to reiterate. "We wouldn't be here if we weren't sure."

"Okay."

Gage gave them one last glance, huddled together, before he slid out of the Jeep and swore to himself that he'd make sure Layla got far away from her fiancé—and that he was going to make things right with Nova. He never should have pulled away from her, never should have put the brakes on with them. Never...messed with her head. He hadn't meant to, but he'd done it all the same. He'd thought he was doing the right thing, but now...she was right. He was a dumbass.

Out in the cold, he nodded once at Burton. "We good to go?" he asked. No reason to bother with pleasantries.

The man nodded once, his expression dark. In his fifties, average height, with dark hair peppered with gray, he'd once been a fighter pilot. According to Skye—who'd used him as an asset of sorts about six years ago—he was a straight arrow who loved his country. "Yeah. Just got a call from another pilot, said some guys are looking for two women. Some bullshit story that a toddler wouldn't believe." He snorted.

"From that direction?" he asked, gesturing to the right where he'd seen those men.

"Yeah."

"You gonna have a problem getting us out of here?"

Burton shook his head then glanced at the Jeep. "This thing hot?"

"Yeah. Can you drop it somewhere, then call it in to the cops later?"

He nodded.

"Good. You ready for us?"

Burton jerked a thumb behind him. "Park it back behind the hangar. Then come in the side door. We'll head over to the Air Yonder Tours hangar."

Gage stilled, ready to draw his weapon. "Where is that? And why are we moving?"

The man's mouth kicked up ever so slightly. "Other side of the airport, and we're moving because of that call I got. I owe Skye. I'll get you guys out of here."

Gage nodded once and headed back to the Jeep. It was time to go home.

* * *

Nausea bubbled up inside Nova as the engine started, the rotors of the helicopter whirring. "Is the whining sound normal?" she asked into the headset. After the plane crash, she didn't mind admitting she was feeling queasy about flying.

"Yep," the pilot said.

All right, then. Gage turned around from the front passenger seat and gave her a reassuring smile. She wondered if he was as nervous as she was to be in a helicopter. The man had been steady as a rock after their plane crash. After he'd landed the dang plane himself. So...yeah, he probably wasn't nervous.

Layla reached out and took her hand, helping to steady her. Jeez, she needed to get it together.

The whining sound tapered off as the rotors spun faster, faster, faster. Her heart rate seemed to increase with the speed of the rotors. Her throat tightened as the pilot did whatever checks he had to do.

"Oh my God!" Layla shouted. "That's Brody!"

Nova turned to look out the window and saw a Land Rover racing toward them at full speed.

"We're leaving now." The pilot's voice was tight, controlled.

Gage pulled out his weapon as the helicopter suddenly lifted into the air. They flew up and forward so suddenly, her stomach jumped into her throat.

Even though they were rising into the air, she had a clear image of Brody Kingston in the passenger seat. It was impossible to see his expression clearly because he had on sunglasses. But it was him.

And he'd figured out where they were.

Her gaze immediately flew to the front of the chopper, but the pilot was maneuvering them higher, higher, as he let out an annoyed curse.

"You got this," Gage muttered, maybe more to himself than anyone.

The pilot made a grunt that could have meant anything as they jerked up—and the glass cracked from a bullet.

Layla screamed even as Nova shoved her to the floor, covering her with her body.

Gage threw open his door and returned fire. *Pop. Pop. Pop.*

One after another, he shot at their attackers. Nova didn't move until he snapped out, "We're clear."

"What about the helicopter?" Nova asked as she sat back up.

"We're fine." Burton's words were clipped. "They didn't hit the rotors or anything mechanical."

Gage turned around and pointed to the ceiling, where a bullet was lodged. *Holy shit.*

They banked left and rose even higher in a sudden twist of direction.

"What about the hole in the window?" she asked, raising her voice because of the whistling—even though he should be able to hear fine with the headsets.

"It's okay. We're—"

"He's going to find me!" Layla was in full-on panic mode, her head between her legs as she took in deep breaths. "And he'll hurt you, Nova! Oh God, I should have never told you any of this."

"He's not going to do a damn thing to us." Nova rubbed her friend's back gently, ignoring the way her own stomach twisted as they soared through the air. "As soon as we get to our rendezvous point, we'll head back home. You'll be safe."

Layla sat up. "Rendezvous point?" Nova shrugged even as Layla's expression relaxed just a bit. Not much, but she didn't seem to be panicking as much. "God, your life is so different from mine. Sorry for freaking out."

"Please, you're allowed."

"How long until we get there?"

"Thirty minutes, max," the pilot answered.

Layla nodded and leaned back against her seat. Nova did the same and glanced at Gage to find him turned around, watching her.

She closed her eyes to block him out. Looking at him just messed with her head, and right now she needed to be a rock for Layla. Because Brody was going to come for them. He wouldn't stop until the Feds got him.

CHAPTER FOURTEEN

—Self-confidence is the best outfit.
Rock it and own it.—

Even though he hated getting on another plane, Gage leaned back in his seat. The Gulfstream was a hell of a lot nicer than what he'd flown on in the Marines.

"What's the deal on the autopsy?" he asked Colt, who sat next to him near the back. Nova and Layla were sitting in the two seats across from them but the others were in the front, talking amongst themselves.

"Waiting on the final report, but it looks like he was given something to knock him out. Found it in his water bottle."

"He was dead before we landed."

Colt's expression was grim. "Maybe he was given too much. Or maybe whatever he was given mixed with his meds wrong—they'll figure it out."

"Where did he get the water from?"

"The pilots' personal stash at the hangar. You already know the transponder was taken—and the plane itself was sabotaged to release fuel."

"So it wasn't exactly random, but Nova and I weren't the targets?"

"Nah. This still leaves us with a problem. The jet was Brooks's, even though we used it. So either he or his father were a target, or the team in general was targeted."

"Get me the details of the sabotage and whatever poison was used. I'll compare it against kills Kuznetsov has been linked to."

"Kuznetsov, really?" Colt's frown grew even deeper.

"It's somewhere to start anyway." The team had come to a truce of sorts with the Russian mobster but Gage didn't think it would last long. "He's not the type of man to let things go. And Brooks has blackmail of sorts on him—and kinda threatened the guy's daughter."

"Even if it's not him, we need to bring him down anyway."

"Yep." Gage kept tabs on the man and nothing had jumped out at him lately. Kuznetsov had his hands busy being an all-around monster. "Hell, I can't see him doing something so random." No, the mobster would use more caution.

"Agreed. So we have a problem until we figure out who was behind the crash."

Gage simply nodded and stifled a laugh as he watched Brooks, Skye and Axel in the front. "Those two are like children," he muttered, not needing to specify who—Colt's wife and Axel. Like kids trapped in adult bodies.

Colt took a sip of his bottled water and shrugged, though his lips curved up slightly. "Yeah."

"I can't believe you put fucking jalapenos in my burrito. You know I hate those. It was like you soaked the damn burrito itself in them." Brooks's expression was annoyed as he spoke to Skye.

Skye lifted an imperious eyebrow. Wearing cargo pants, a long-sleeved shirt—everything black—and strapped down in a plethora of weapons, she looked as she normally did, ready to go into battle. "I *did* soak the tortilla in the juice! Maybe you shouldn't have messed with the settings on my office chair."

"You never sit in the damn thing. I just readjusted it for my height!"

"Doesn't matter. It's still *mine*. You have to respect the sanctity of my office."

"Like you respect the sanctity of my kitchen?" Brooks asked.

"I clean up after myself. Besides, I know what this is really about. You're just mad about the bachelor party." She smirked knowingly.

Next to her, Axel snorted to cover a laugh.

Brooks turned to him. "We're going to be family soon. You're supposed to take my side."

Axel simply lifted an arm and silently fist-bumped Skye. "Nope. My best woman's got my loyalty."

Brooks rolled his eyes before turning to Skye. "I'm not pissed about the bachelor party. If anything, you should be scared because I'm gonna kick your ass at the range."

"What the hell is going on with the bachelor party?" Gage murmured to Colt, still half listening to the three of them up front. Axel was marrying Hadley soon— Brooks's younger sister—and since Skye was the "best woman," she was in charge of all things bachelor party related.

"Skye rented out a local shooting range and we're all going to compete with each other. She's got something ridiculous set up for the prizes. Gift baskets of ammo— and I wish I was kidding, but I'm not. She's been making them up on her own and they're strewn all over our dining room table. And she made a bet with Brooks that she could kick his ass in pistols."

Gage simply shook his head. Brooks had been a sniper in the Marine Corps, so it would take someone seriously special to beat him, no matter how good all the rest of them were with weapons. Though Skye was pretty skilled. "Skye is very sure of herself."

"That's true. My woman does not lack in confidence."

"Neither do you," Gage murmured before he could censor himself.

"What?" Colt shot him a sideways glance.

He lifted a shoulder. "The two of them, Axel and Skye," he said, tilting his chin toward them. "It seriously doesn't bother you how tight they are?"

Colt lifted a shoulder. "At first, for like a day, maybe. But no. Skye is mine. I'm all in with her, one hundred percent, and that means I trust her. Just as she trusts me. Those two... In a way, they're both outsiders. Not really, but they didn't grow up with us, and...it's hard for Skye to make friends. You think I'm going to get pissed when she's finally added someone new to her tribe? Nah. I could never take that away. It would hurt her, and I'd rather eat my own arm than do that."

Well when he put it that way, it made a lot of sense. And it made Gage feel small. "I just don't know if…" He trailed off.

"What?"

"Nothing." He wasn't going to tell anyone about what had happened with him and Nova. Not yet anyway. Not until he could convince her that he'd just been acting like a dumbass and that he wanted more from her. Hell, he wanted *everything* from her. While he might not be as relaxed as Colt if Nova ever developed such a close relationship with someone of the opposite sex, he knew he wanted what Colt and Skye had.

And not just with anyone. He wanted it with Nova. He'd fallen in lust with her voice before he'd even met her. Then when he finally met her in person, she'd knocked him on his ass with that sassy attitude. There wasn't anyone else for him. And he shouldn't have pushed her away.

He glanced across the aisle to find her and Layla both still sleeping. Their heads were tilted toward each other as they leaned against each other. She looked so peaceful sleeping.

Good. She needed the rest. She'd put on a strong front, but he knew she was exhausted and, more than that, scared for her friend. He just wished she was leaning on him right now. That he had the right and the privilege of being the shoulder she leaned on.

No matter what, they'd make sure Layla was taken care of. And if the Feds couldn't do their job, he'd make sure Brody Kingston disappeared forever. Because if he was alive, he'd be a threat to Nova—the woman who'd helped Layla escape. Gage didn't relish going that route, but if it came down to it, he'd do what was necessary.

CHAPTER FIFTEEN

—No one is perfect.
That's why pencils have erasers.—

"Thanks for doing this," Leighton said to Hazel, fighting the awkwardness burning inside him. He tried not to think about the last time he'd seen her and how much he'd embarrassed himself. She wasn't at Brooks's ranch for him, she was here in an official capacity.

As Special Agent Hazel Blake.

She nodded once, her expression serious as usual, but there was something else there that he couldn't stand. Something that made him want to crawl inside himself. Pity.

"I'm glad you called. Ms. Ferrer seems like she's got a level head. She's been through a lot and she's emotional, as you'd expect, but she's going to come through this okay."

"Good. Good." He inwardly winced as he repeated himself. *Way to make normal conversation, jackass*, he inwardly chastised himself. He and Hazel had been friends a long time. He had to get over this—to make things right.

"Look, I need to head back in there and go over a few things with her, but...can I say something?"

He nodded once.

"I don't want there to be any weirdness between us. I know a little bit is inevitable, but I'm not what you want."

He let out a laugh with no humor. "Is that right?"

"Yeah, that *is* right. Even if I didn't have a girlfriend right now, that's right. You're looking for something but it's not me. You haven't even told me what happened overseas, whatever it was that changed you. And I'm not asking. Obviously if you want to talk, I'm always here for you. Always. As a friend. But the point is, if you'd wanted something between us, you would have opened up more. The only reason you made a move on me is because I'm comfortable. Not because you can't live without me, not because there's any sort of epic chemistry between us. Don't even try to pretend otherwise. You were simply drunk and feeling sorry for yourself the other night."

He gritted his teeth for a long moment as he digested her words. Her very correct words. "I seriously hate it when you're right."

She snorted. "Then you must hate being around me a lot of the time."

A laugh escaped and, though he felt rusty at it, it felt good. "I'm sorry I tried to kiss you," he muttered, still inwardly cursing himself. He'd had one too many beers, and she'd been in town for a job so she'd met up with them. And he'd made a complete ass of himself and tried to kiss one of his friends. One of his oldest friends—besides the people he'd grown up with.

"Please tell me things will be normal between us." There was a sort of desperation in her voice that surprised him. Then she continued, "I don't have a lot of true friends. Not the kind like you, that I can depend on. If I call and ask you to help me hide a body, I know you'll be there."

"I swear it won't be weird. I was apparently having a moment of insanity. I don't know what the hell is wrong with me." That wasn't exactly true, but he didn't want to tell her what was wrong with him, what had been weighing on his mind for years. Ever since that day in Afghanistan.

"You sure you don't want to talk about it?"

He paused then nodded. "Yeah, I'm sure. I just need to work through some shit." Too bad he'd been trying to work through it for years—and nothing helped.

"Okay, then."

"How's Melissa?" he asked, really wanting to know. He'd never seen Hazel so happy.

At the mention of her new girlfriend, Hazel's cheeks flushed as she smiled. "She's perfect. I think she's the one. Something I never thought I'd say." Hazel had fallen for a sweet kindergarten teacher who taught yoga on the side. The complete opposite of Hazel, who was an all-around badass.

"Good. You deserve to be happy."

"It's weird. I guess I just always assumed that when I decided to settle down—if I ever did—it would be with someone more like me. Then I met Melissa and..." She shrugged. "I knew. She's so damn kind and giving."

Leighton hoped it worked out. Hazel had a tough job and did a lot of good—and was just a good person. She was the kind of person who made the world a better place, and he was happy she wasn't holding his stupidity against him. "Just make sure I'm invited to the wedding."

She laughed. "As if that would be in question. Hell, you'll probably be *in* the wedding. I know I've said it before but I'll say it again—I love what you guys are doing. I love this whole crew," she said, subtly changing the subject. "Thank you for reaching out to me about Ms. Ferrer."

"Of course. I trust you more than most people."

She stepped forward and pulled him into a hug. "Whatever the hell is going on with you, talk to a therapist," she rasped out as she held him close. "Or talk to someone. I don't care who. Don't bottle that shit up."

Dammit, she had always seen through him. Throat tight, he simply nodded and then returned her hug before stepping back. "Get back in there. I know you've got a job to do."

As Hazel stepped out of the downstairs office and headed back to where her partner was waiting with Layla and Nova, Leighton shut the door behind her and sat in one of the chairs. The office was generic. Tastefully decorated, of course, but boring all the same. No one ever used this room as far as he was aware of. But who really knew. Brooks's estate was gigantic—too much space. He rubbed a hand over his face and ordered himself to get it together. He had stuff to do.

Always something to do. This new job was what kept him sane, what kept him from spending too much time alone with his thoughts. Memories.

Guilt.

Maybe Hazel was right. Maybe he did need to talk to someone. He didn't want to tell any of his friends what he'd done. Or rather, what he hadn't done. Because it shamed him too deeply. He didn't care if he'd just been following orders. There were some things he simply couldn't take back.

* * *

Gage opened the office door and stuck his head inside, surprised Leighton was sitting there alone. "Hey, what are you doing? I thought Hazel would be with you." Which was the whole reason he was here right now.

Leighton shrugged and stood. "What's up?" he asked, not exactly answering. "Hazel's in with the women."

"You sure she's solid for this?" Gage probably shouldn't have asked that, considering what Hazel had done for them in the past, but he was on a razor's edge of control.

Leighton's eyes narrowed ever so slightly. "You're seriously going to ask me that after all she's done for us?"

"We've done a lot for her too." She'd gotten promoted after taking credit for stopping a bombing that they'd actually prevented.

"True enough. But you know her. Don't be a dick."

Gage paused once then shoved his hands in his pockets. "You're right. I'm sorry. I just hate that Nova is dealing with all this. I hate that her friend is likely going to have to leave. I just...hate it all." And he was helpless, which made it even harder. The Feds were taking over now, which was better for everyone, but that wouldn't make things better for Nova. Because unfortunately, Layla would be leaving very soon. They'd want to put her in a safe house, maybe even WITSEC—because Hazel had told them the marshals were en route. And there was only one reason they were coming to town.

The tension in Leighton's shoulders eased and he nodded in understanding. "No worries, man. I get it. If I was in love with someone and—"

"Love?"

Leighton snorted. "Fine, whatever. If I was 'into someone' and she was going through this shit, I'd be a cranky dick right now too. And we all know how you feel about Nova."

"What exactly do you think you know?" He hadn't told a soul about what had happened between them in Montana, and she'd been distant with him since they'd stepped foot on the jet. Not distant in a cold way, just polite and almost formal.

"Please. I know your dumbass self—she's it for you."

"Is that like my new nickname now?" he muttered. He only liked it when Nova called him a dumbass. She got this adorable, completely exasperated look on her face when she said it. And it made him want to kiss her senseless every single time. Of course, he usually wanted to kiss her.

"Hey, if the shoe fits..." Leighton grinned, and the sight was so rare it made Gage smile to himself.

"Well...thank Hazel again for what she's done." He planned to be waiting outside the room where the Feds were talking to the women. He wanted to be there for Nova. If things went down like he thought they would, he was pretty sure Layla would be leaving soon.

"I will. But she knows. And I'm going to give you some unsolicited advice. Don't wait too long to get over whatever you need to get over with Nova. Because she's a catch. And you should have made a move long before now."

A surge of jealousy sparked inside him. "You think I don't know that?"

Leighton simply shook his head, his grin growing—and again, the sight of that amusement on Leighton's face was so out of the ordinary that it startled Gage. He'd missed seeing his friend smile. "I can't believe you're actually jealous. Just don't wait too long. Life's too short." At that, Leighton left the office.

Gage knew it was true. He also knew he was going to do something about his own stubbornness as soon as he had time alone with Nova. Not tonight, because he knew she'd want to spend it with her friend.

But hell, it had to be soon. He needed to tell her how he felt, admit that he'd been wrong. That he wanted something real between them—something exclusive. Because he didn't think he could let Nova go. She'd branded him, and he would always belong to her.

CHAPTER SIXTEEN

—Embrace the suck.—

N ova reached over and squeezed Layla's hand as Special Agent Hazel Blake and her partner, Neil Harvey, sat in front of them. Hazel's jet-black hair was pulled back into a low ponytail, her expression open and friendly. Her partner wore a plain dark suit, was likely in his thirties, and in good shape. He had that same open expression as Hazel. Nova wondered if it was real or just what they did to put people at ease.

"Thank you for all you've done to come forward with this information," Hazel said, her gaze on Layla. "I understand why you were hesitant to reach out to the DEA because of what you saw—and you were smart to come to us first."

Layla simply nodded. They'd been in one of the sitting rooms in Brooks's gigantic house for the last couple hours since arriving in Redemption Harbor. This was Layla's safe house for now.

Nova was actually surprised the Feds hadn't taken them to a generic-looking building and stuck them in some stuffy, windowless room, but apparently Brooks, or maybe Leighton, had pulled some strings. Not to mention the Feds really wanted to bring down Brody

Kingston. Well, bring him down and find out who he was working with, because apparently he had a large network of people who insulated him from law enforcement. Including some dirty law enforcement officials.

"All of this is overwhelming, but I know what I saw. And I will testify against him." Layla might be scared, but she'd regained her strength and was ready to move forward with whatever she had to do.

Nova could only imagine how hard all this was. Her best friend had seen the man she loved murder someone, and then learned that he trafficked drugs and people. That was a lot for anyone to take in.

"From this point forward, I'm going to be working in tandem with the marshals," Hazel said. "It's a possibility they'll put you into WITSEC eventually and, if that happens, things will shift slightly."

Layla squeezed Nova's hand but didn't say anything, just nodded at the agent. They'd already talked about this possibility on the plane. Nova hated the thought of her friend disappearing, and never seeing her again and only getting to communicate sporadically. But she was being selfish, so she shoved those thoughts aside. Right now wasn't about her. It was about getting justice for a man who'd just been doing his job, a man who'd left family behind, including two little girls. Not to mention all the other people Kingston hurt.

"I can give you one more night here, because this place is secure and the marshals are en route now. It doesn't make sense to move you just to move you again in the morning."

"You trust these guys?" Nova asked. "The marshals?"

Hazel nodded. "I picked them out myself. People I've worked directly with before. And we've got some images for you to look at to see if you can identify the DEA agent you saw with your ex-fiancé the day he murdered the other agent."

"I'll never forget his face."

"You've already given us enough details and the marshals have a sketch artist as well. But that's only necessary if you can't identify the man through pictures."

"Where's Brody now?" Layla asked.

The agent shook her head. "He's gone to ground. No one knows where he is. We've got guys on his house and other known holdings, and he hasn't surfaced anywhere. After the shootout at the airport, he basically disappeared. By the time the locals got there, he and his guys were gone. But no one can disappear forever. We'll find him."

"Okay." Layla didn't sound convinced.

"Trust me. He's not going to get to you. The marshals are very good at their job. We'll get you into a safe house. Nothing as nice as this," she said, laughing slightly and easing the tension in the room. "But it will be nice, and from there we'll figure out what to do. And there's a possibility you won't go into WITSEC. It just depends on how all of this plays out, whether he decides to make a deal or if you even need to testify at all."

Layla shook her head sharply. "No matter what, he's going to want to kill me. He won't forgive me for betraying him. And that's how he'll view what I'm doing—as a betrayal."

The expression on Hazel's face said she agreed with her. But she simply nodded once at her partner and they stood together. Then she held out a hand to both women. "Thank you for helping to get your friend here," she said to Nova.

Nova just shrugged. Like there had been any other option.

Once the agents left the room, Layla collapsed back against the couch. "All of this feels so surreal."

Tears stung Nova's eyes as she twisted toward her friend, leaning her elbow against the back of the couch. "I wish you could just stay here." An impossibility of course, but she didn't want Layla to leave.

"No kidding. I could easily live here. You could fit ten families in this place."

Nova snorted softly. "They have an actual movie room."

Layla's eyes widened slightly. "Are you serious?"

"Yep. Totally serious. Big screen, comfy recliners, the whole works."

"You think we could watch a movie tonight?"

They could do anything Layla wanted, as long as they didn't leave the place.

Before Nova could respond, Brooks and Gage stepped into the room. Brooks said, "You can watch anything you want. And I've got some vintage bottles of wine here that you're more than welcome to enjoy. I know you've been through a lot."

At Brooks's words, Layla started crying, as if something broke inside her.

Hell. Nova forced back her own tears because she wanted to be strong for her friend, but she pulled her into her arms and let Layla cry for all that she was losing. Leaving her entire life behind, no matter how strong she was, was going to be incredibly difficult. Nova wasn't sure she could do it.

The men left them alone and she avoided looking at Gage. She didn't have the strength or energy to deal with him right now.

"Well, I think I'm okay now." Layla's voice was watery as she pulled back and swiped at her face. "And I'm totally going to take advantage of that man's wine because you know it's got to be good. Maybe he'll even let me take one on the road."

Nova let out a startled laugh. Now that was classic Layla. And in that moment, she knew her best friend would be okay no matter where she ended up. But she was going to miss her something fierce.

CHAPTER SEVENTEEN

—Bitches get stuff done.—

Fourteen years ago

Nova bolted upright from the lounge chair as a shadow fell across her and a male voice said, "Damn, girl." Then he continued with, "Who are you?" He was some guy she vaguely recognized from school. His name was Marco something and he was seventeen— maybe. He wasn't in her grade, that much she knew.

She quickly grabbed her beach towel and wrapped it around herself as she jumped to her feet, the overgrown grass thick between her toes. "None of your business. Who are you?" she snapped out.

Her foster mom was at the grocery store so she and her new friend/foster sister, Layla, had planned to get some sun in the backyard. Her real sister, Rosaleigh, was off who knew where, but Layla had said she'd be right back.

The guy's eyes narrowed at her, his expression one she recognized well. She'd seen it on some of her mom's boyfriends. *Anger.* So, this dude was quick to anger. *Great.* She wondered if all men were like this because it sure as hell seemed like it. Although, this guy wasn't a man. He was a boy. Still, he was bigger than her and she was very aware of how alone she was right now. A little tingle started at the base of her skull, telling her to put distance between herself and this guy.

She risked a quick glance at the back door, looking for Layla. They were the same age and Layla wasn't any bigger than her, but two people were better than one. She'd learned that most people wouldn't do anything when there were witnesses around.

"Where's Mrs. Baker?" the guy asked, shoving his hands into his shorts pockets.

"Sleeping, I guess. I'm not her keeper." She figured giving as little information as possible was good right now. She lifted a shoulder as if she didn't care either way. But the truth was, she wished Mrs. Baker was here right now. The older woman was kind of annoying, but she also had kind eyes and didn't seem to put up with much crap from anyone.

"She's got all my stuff and I'm here for it."

Oh, he must be one of her former foster kids. Layla had mentioned that someone else had lived her right before Nova and Rosaleigh moved in, but the guy had been removed because he liked to break stuff. Must be this guy.

Turning away from her when she didn't respond, he started for the back door.

Alarm punched through her. "You can't just go in there. You have to wait until she gets back."

He swiveled on her, his eyes narrowing. This time there wasn't anger in his expression but something she also recognized from some of her mom's boyfriends. He was looking at her as if she was undressed even though she had the towel wrapped around her. Now she was cursing herself for wearing a bikini. Not that it would've mattered. Guys like this were gross and wouldn't care if she'd been in a full-length dress with long sleeves.

"I thought you said she was sleeping."

"No, I said I'm not her keeper. You should go knock on the front door like a normal person. Why the hell are you even in her backyard? You can't just go inside her house."

He took a step closer until he was towering over her, his huge body blocking her from escape. The backyard wasn't that big but she had a feeling that if she screamed for help, no one would come. This wasn't that kind of neighborhood. It wasn't bad exactly but people minded their own business, and even though it was Saturday, most people were working. In her experience, only middle class and rich people got weekends off.

Ice fingers slithered down her spine as she tried to make herself look taller. She wasn't going to cower before this guy.

"I can do whatever the hell I want," he said quietly, his voice pure menace.

Okay, new plan. She was going to make a run for it. If she could get to the front yard, she'd have a better chance of being seen by someone.

As if he sensed what she was going to do, or maybe he just read her expression, his big hand shot out and wrapped around her throat as he shoved her to the ground.

He fell on top of her, forcing all the air from her lungs. She lifted her knee, trying to hit him in the dick, but he just laughed as he clawed at her towel.

Everything around her funneled out as she realized what he intended. Tears burned her eyes as she grasped at his hand, trying to get him to stop choking her, when suddenly he screamed in pain, rolling off her.

"Get the hell off her!" Layla screamed, lifting a bat, slamming it into Marco's back—again.

The guy writhed onto the ground screaming and Layla jabbed him in the stomach.

He rolled over and dry heaved. "Bitch," he wheezed out.

"That's right I am!" Layla shouted as Nova struggled to her feet. "If you come around here again I'll call the cops. I know you've been in juvie too many times and you turn eighteen in a month. See what happens if you come back here! You think you'll survive in jail, mother-fucker!"

The guy paled and stumbled from the backyard, holding on to his stomach as he moved as fast as he could.

Nova stared at her friend in shock and a little awe. "Motherfucker?"

Letting out a shaky smile, Layla shrugged. "That guy's a jerk. I'm just speaking his language. Oh my God, are you okay?"

Nova nodded, and rubbed her throat, hoping it wouldn't bruise. "Yeah. Did he ever hurt you? Before?"

Layla shook her head. "No, but I didn't like the way he looked at me. We were only in the house together for like a week. They were in the process of moving him and he was always super creepy."

"Do you think he'll come back?"

Layla shook her head. "Nah. That guy's a loser. And I wasn't kidding, he will be eighteen soon. If he's completely mental, he'll come back but I kind of doubt it. And if he does…" She lifted her bat and jabbed it into the ground next to her.

Nova giggled at Layla's ferocity—the petite Puerto Rican looked so innocent—but almost immediately started crying as she thought about what would have happened.

Layla tugged her into her arms. "Don't let that moron make you cry. He's garbage."

Nova hadn't been in foster care for very long and she was so grateful to have found a friend like Layla. Even though her mom wasn't the best parent, at least with some things it was better when it was the devil you knew. Less than a month ago she and her sister had been thrust into this whole new world and everything was terrifying. But Layla seemed so cool and confident.

"Seriously, don't waste any tears on the douchebag." Layla stepped back and picked up her bat again. "You still want to lay out?"

Nova shook her head. "Not really." She felt too vulnerable to be out there in her bikini right now.

"Okay, let's head down to Dairy Queen. I'm hungry anyway."

"Should we wait for Mrs. Baker?"

Layla snorted. "Hell no. She said she was going grocery shopping but she's really going to play bingo so she won't be back for a while."

"Okay." Being dropped into foster care so suddenly had been scary. Nova was so glad she'd met Layla.

CHAPTER EIGHTEEN

—Always go for the second orgasm.—

"I would ask how you're doing but I think I know the answer," Gage said, sliding onto the barstool next to her.

Nova didn't look up from her coffee because if she looked at him, she'd probably get emotional. And she figured she'd done enough of that in the last couple days.

"The marshals came earlier than I expected." They'd gotten to the house at eight o'clock sharp and had whisked Layla away with no fanfare.

"She'll be safe, and Hazel promised to keep us updated."

"I know. Still doesn't make it any easier."

When Gage's big, warm hand settled on her shoulder, she abruptly stood. She seriously could not deal with him right now. Not his comfort or his annoyingly handsome face.

"Nova," he said as her chair squeaked against the tile floor.

She kept her face diverted away from him, unable to meet his gaze. "Gage, I'm exhausted."

"I know, and I don't want to add to it. I just want to say…I was a jackass. Everything I said back in Montana, I was wrong."

Okay, that had her attention. She turned to look at him, pinned him with a hard gaze. "Is this you feeling sorry for me?"

Shaking his head, he stood abruptly. She was just wearing jeans, a sweater and no shoes, so he actually towered over her for once. "I do feel bad about what's going on, but that's not what this is about. When we were running from those guys, when I told you to leave me if anything happened to me, I saw in your eyes that you wouldn't leave. And I realized that I am the biggest dumbass in the world."

She wrapped her arms around herself. "If you're looking for an argument from me, you're not going to get one. You gave me some stupid logic about why we couldn't be together. Then you screwed with my head."

He shoved his hands in his pockets and had started to say something when Skye strolled into the kitchen in full-on jogging gear, earbuds in and a banana in her hand. She took one look at the two of them, then turned right back around.

Okay, then.

"Come on." Gage gently took Nova's elbow and guided them to the nearest door and stepped into what turned out to be a laundry room.

A laundry room that was twice the size of her master bathroom at home. This thing was ridiculous. Shutting the door behind them, he turned to face her again.

Standing in that room with Gage, she felt vulnerable. She wasn't worried that he'd hurt her, not physically at least. But she had no idea where he was going with this.

"I thought I was in love once," he said abruptly. "It was stupid, and I got that clichéd Dear John letter. It kinda messed me up because I'd fallen for her. I thought she was out of my league. I couldn't believe she'd fallen for me, not when I have friends that look like Brooks."

Nova frowned at his words. "You're a catch—you're the smartest man I know! You're also funny, respectful, and sexy." Sooooo very sexy.

But he seemed somehow surprised by her words. He rubbed the back of his neck. "You can say that all you want, but…I don't know. Sometimes I wonder what you see in me."

"You mean besides everything I just told you?" Her voice was dry.

He laughed, seeming startled with himself. "It's no wonder I fell for you."

"Wait… You've fallen for me?"

He stepped closer, cupping her cheek with one big hand. She leaned into it, rubbing against his callused palm. "How could I not? I can't get enough of you. I know what I said before about the issue of us working together."

"So you admit that it's bullshit?" She stepped closer, wrapping her arms around his waist as she looked up at him.

"No, I still believe all that stuff. If something were to happen to us and we didn't work out—"

"Why wouldn't we work out?"

"Because you're going to figure out you can do better than me?" he asked jokingly, but she had a feeling he wasn't kidding at all.

She pinched his side. "You don't get to talk about yourself like that." They watched each other for a long moment, blood rushing in her ears as she stared into his bluish-gray eyes. Finally she said, "So...what do you want? I need it spelled out."

"I want to be with you." His grip on her tightened. "Just you. As in, a relationship. And I won't share."

She snorted softly. "Neither will I, so we're on the same page. And...I'm clean and on the pill." She figured they might as well get that all out in the open now. Because they would be having sex soon, no doubt.

His eyes went molten hot. "I'm clean too. Tested and haven't been with anyone in...a while."

Her lips curved up. "Good. I'd also like you to admit that I am the queen of everything and if you hadn't been such a dumbass, we could have been doing *this* for the last few months." She leaned up on tiptoe to brush her lips over his, but he took over immediately, deepening the kiss as his grip tightened on her hip.

He slid his other hand through her hair, cupping the back of her skull as she moaned into his mouth. She wanted to jump him right here in the laundry room. To let him hoist her up on the nearest surface and go to town.

When he suddenly pulled away, she leaned into him, wanting to tug him right back. "We should probably stop unless you want me inside you in the next few minutes."

Her inner walls tightened at the whole sexy growl thing he had going on. The thought of him being inside her soon? Yes, please. But...yeah, not here. "Well, I'm not doing it in a laundry room where anyone might walk in, so how about we head to the nearest bedroom." She was done waiting, wondering—fantasizing about him. Yeah, he could still break her heart, but she wasn't one to live her life afraid to take chances.

Gage blinked once, his entire body going still in an almost preternatural way. But he quickly recovered and rolled his hips against her. And she felt his reaction clearly as he pulled her completely against him and crushed his mouth to hers once again. So maybe they would be getting busy in the laundry room after all.

She arched into him, her body molding against his as they got lost in one another. It was impossible to think of anything else when he slid his hand up the back of her sweater, his rough fingers teasing against her skin. She didn't care about the location anymore. Here was fine. God, they both had way too many clothes on.

"Ahem."

Nova drew back sharply to find Douglas Alexander standing in the doorway, an amused expression on his face. She hadn't even heard the door open. Clearly neither had Gage, which said a whole lot about where his head was because that man had serious awareness.

"Mr. Alexander," she started, then didn't know how to finish. What was she going to do, apologize for...what? Making out with Gage? She was a grown woman.

Gage took her hand and murmured an apology to the older man before he pulled her out of the room. Maybe it was a little rude and a lot awkward, but it saved her from having an uncomfortable conversation with someone she genuinely liked.

Somehow she didn't think he really cared, because she heard the older man's muted laughter as Gage dragged her from the room.

"Where are we going?" she murmured as they headed through the kitchen.

"Bedroom."

Okay, that left open questions, like whose bedroom? Not that she actually cared. As they reached one of the staircases, she was glad Gage clearly knew where they were going. She always got confused in this sprawling place. Once they reached the top of the stairs, he started to tug her to the right.

Colt stepped out of one of the bedrooms and opened his mouth when he saw them.

Whatever he was about to say was cut off when Gage snapped, "Unless someone is on fire, I don't care. Don't bother us!"

Colt blinked once, then grinned, and Nova felt her cheeks heat up, but she really didn't care what anyone thought. So what if everyone found out she and Gage were...

Holy hell, he was her boyfriend. Which felt weird to think. And they were about to have sex—which was *not* weird to think. Just hot.

When they reached one of the doors, Gage barreled on through like a man possessed, and yeah, it was super-hot. "You are definitely the queen of everything," he growled out before pressing her up against the bedroom door.

It took her a second before it registered that he was referring to what she'd said in the laundry room. Before she could respond, she heard the click of the lock behind her and then his mouth was on hers.

Hot and hungry.

Demanding and dominating.

He was devouring her as he kept her pinned up against the door. She loved every second of it. Heck, she loved *him*, even if she wasn't ready to say it yet.

She also loved the way he kept her in place, his fingers tangled in her hair as he cupped the back of her head. The way he kissed her, it was as if he were starving and she was his sustenance.

Heat pooled between her legs with each tease and stroke of his tongue. It was too much and not enough.

She'd been fantasizing about this for what felt like forever, and now whatever had been holding him back before was gone. Destroyed. There was nothing dividing them anymore.

"Naked," she moaned out against his mouth. He needed to be naked right now.

He pulled back, his bluish-gray eyes heavy-lidded. "Naked?"

"You. Now. Naked." And that was about all she could get out.

Without a word, he tugged his sweater over his head, revealing the bare chest she'd fantasized about. A few faint scars nicked his pecs and abs, but before she'd had a chance to enjoy every single inch, he went for his belt.

Aaaaand she lost the ability to process anything as he quickly divested himself of his pants—and she discovered he went commando. Oh, sweet flying puppies.

He. Went. *Commando.*

His thick cock curved upward, resting against his lower abdomen, just begging for her to touch. Reaching for him, she started to wrap her fingers around his length, but he scooped her up.

"Now I get to undress *you.*" There was a wicked promise in his words, one she felt all the way to her core.

She froze for about a second. "Me?" She was still drinking in the sight of Gage, the most beautiful man in the world.

"That's right," he murmured as he stretched her out on the huge bed. It vaguely registered that they must be in his bedroom. Or she really hoped they were. At least he'd locked the door, so if this was someone else's room, they wouldn't be interrupted. And right now, nothing and no one could stop her.

"I've fantasized about doing this since you told me to learn some manners and then hung up on me." His eyes blazed with undeniable lust.

"You'd never even seen me then," she whispered. She remembered that conversation well. He'd been rude to her, so she'd told him that once he'd learned the manners he should have in kindergarten, to feel free to call back. He had called back, and his voice had been all butter-smooth politeness.

"Didn't matter. Your voice drives me crazy," he growled out. "After our first conversation, I jerked off to the memory of your voice later."

It was the first time anyone had ever told her that. Normally she was told that she was too much of a smart-ass or too much of something. But not to Gage. To him, she was perfect. And vice versa.

She stretched out on the bed, and though she wasn't feeling patient, she forced herself to relax as he slowly reached for the button of her jeans. Part of her felt guilty for enjoying herself right now when her friend was being put into a safe house, but she shoved all of that down into a little box in her mind. She had a right to enjoy this, to enjoy Gage.

Life was so damn short. Too short. And she was pretty sure that after surviving a plane crash, they'd earned this.

His gaze landed on the juncture of her thighs as he tossed her jeans away. "I'd hoped you wouldn't be wearing anything underneath," he murmured.

Heat flooded her at his words, thick and heavy. "I'll remember that for next time." She'd never been one to go commando, but she'd make an exception for Gage. And there would be a next time. Many, many times. No doubt about it. She was going to grab on to this man and never let go.

Gage felt as if he were coming apart at the seams as he stared at Nova stretched out on the bed. He wished it was his bed at home, where they had all the privacy in the world, but that would happen soon enough. Once it was safe.

She looked like a goddess with her dark hair everywhere, her eyes heavy-lidded as she stared up at him with raw hunger. Something he'd only imagined from her. He needed her completely naked before he tasted her. And taste her he would.

Though it took self-control, he managed to get her shirt off without ripping it. He wanted to take his time with her, to do things right. Though he had been sorely tempted to take her right up against the bedroom door.

When she was finally, thankfully, naked in front of him, he knew that this was absolute heaven, right here, right now. "You're incredible," he managed to rasp out, his throat scratchy.

In response, she slightly lifted her hips, a silent invitation.

Fuuuuuck yes. She didn't have to ask him for anything. He wanted her hands and mouth all over him, but he wanted to go first—had to. If he'd thought his fantasies could compare with the reality, he realized how wrong he was in that moment. Because nothing compared to the reality of Nova. Perfect, all his, Nova. Crawling up her body, he covered her again, caging her in, his cock heavy between their bodies as he crushed his mouth to hers.

She tasted like sweet perfection. Like *his.* She arched into him, her full breasts rubbing against his chest, her nipples hard. He'd never actually thought this would happen, that she would be in his arms like this, just as desperate for him as he was for her. Apparently miracles happened.

Though he hated pulling away from her, for even a second, he drew back slightly, nipped her bottom lip. Then he continued downward, gently kissing her throat, breasts, anywhere he could touch. And he reveled in every little moan she made.

It was nearly enough to make his brain overload. She was so damn reactive to his every touch. He wanted to kiss her everywhere all at once, to consume her. Just as she'd consumed him since the moment they'd met.

198 | KATIE REUS

When he buried his face between her legs, he oh so gently teased her clit. He wasn't sure how sensitive she'd be, and she nearly jolted off the bed as he flicked his tongue over the sensitive bundle of nerves.

He groaned against her, wanting to drown in her.

"Gage," she moaned out his name. She said it like a prayer, the word begging and reverent at the same time.

He growled against her slick folds, the sound of his name on her lips making him feel absolutely possessed with the need to claim her. He knew it was too soon, but he wanted a ring on her finger. He wanted every man to know she was off-limits, that she belonged to him. He felt like a barbarian but he didn't care.

Nova was everything to him. The world needed to know it.

He dipped a finger between her folds, groaning as her tight walls clenched around him. Soon it wouldn't just be his finger. And at that thought, his balls pulled up impossibly tight.

She was so damn wet. And it was all for him. All because of him.

"More," she half begged, half demanded.

His cock jerked at her tone and he added another finger, though he wasn't sure that was what she wanted. But he was going to learn her body, learn everything she loved and bring her so much pleasure. He'd never felt like this about anyone. All he wanted to do was give her anything and everything she wanted.

As he began moving his fingers in and out of her in a slow rhythm, she moaned out his name again, her hips rolling against his thrusts.

He continued teasing her clit, increasing pressure with each strangled sound she made. When her fingers dug into his scalp, he knew she was close. Good, he wanted her to come at least once before he was inside her.

Then he was going to make her come again. He wanted her completely addicted to him.

Because he might not have been inside her yet, but he was already addicted to *her*. Nova, his not-so-secret addiction and drug of choice. Walking, talking sex appeal.

Her thighs tightened around his head even as he knew her orgasm was starting. Taking him off guard, it crested fast and sharp as a cry tore from her throat.

"Oh, fuck," she shouted.

Primal satisfaction surged through him as her orgasm punched through her, her slickness coating his fingers as she rolled her hips against his face, completely uninhibited.

As she came down from her high, he moved up her body, caging her in with his arms as he brushed his lips over hers. His hard length was heavy between his legs, teasing her lips, but before he had a chance to ask if this was what she really wanted, she shifted up and impaled herself on him.

"Nova," he groaned.

She was so damn tight, and he savored the sensation of her inner walls clamping around him. He wanted to stay like this, to memorize it.

But he had to move. Now. As he thrust inside her once, twice, she met him stroke for stroke, grabbing onto his shoulders and gripping him tight.

As he looked into her eyes, he knew that she was it for him. For always.

She'd been the one for him from practically the moment they'd met, he just hadn't realized it until today.

He could see his whole future with her. A woman who would always have his back. The woman he wanted to have kids with, make a real life with, put down serious roots with.

Nova was his North Star.

He kissed her again, his tongue teasing hers, feverish in his need as their bodies joined, over and over, completely lost in her. Drowning in her.

His own orgasm was coming up hard, but he desperately wanted her to climax again. He wanted to feel her walls clamping down on his cock as he brought her more pleasure.

Reaching between their bodies, he teased her clit, adding more pressure than before. It didn't take long for her to climax again.

"Gage!"

That was all it took for his control to completely snap.

He buried his face against her neck, inhaling that sweet scent as he came inside her in hard strokes.

This was definitely heaven, and better than anything he'd ever fantasized about.

He loved her. He knew without a doubt.

But he bit back the words even as he lost himself inside her. Because he didn't want to scare her off. No way.

He was going to do this right, get her addicted to him before she realized it—then lock her down for life.

CHAPTER NINETEEN

—In the end, karma is the most badass bitch of all.—

Brody wanted to shove his fist through someone's face, but he managed to keep his cool. He'd made his way to Redemption Harbor and was now holed up in some basic rental home on the outskirts of town with a guy he used for research and hacking. It was the only place he could think to find his missing fiancée since she'd left with that bitch best friend of hers.

Nova Blaire. She was definitely going to die.

"She couldn't have just disappeared," he snapped to Sam Oliver, the man he'd brought with him for his hacking skills. Oliver should have found Layla by now—because she wasn't that sophisticated. There's no way she could have just gone dark like this.

Oliver didn't look up from his laptop. "She could have if she went to the Feds."

"Layla wouldn't have done that. She would not have betrayed me." But even as he said the words, he didn't believe them. Not anymore. At first he'd tried to convince himself that she'd been taken by Nova and whoever that other guy had been. The guy who'd shot at his men.

Oliver snorted as his fingers moved over the keyboard. "Are you sure about that?"

"I've given her everything she could ever want." She'd been a teacher before him. A *teacher*. She'd spent her day with annoying, whiny kids. Pathetic.

But...as he thought about the last couple weeks, he knew that something had shifted. It hadn't been overt, and he'd assumed she was simply nervous about the wedding. It was going to be bigger than she'd wanted and she'd complained about that. But nothing had seemed out of the ordinary, not her texts, not her emails, nothing. He knew because he checked up on her religiously— had to make sure she never stepped out on him.

Everything had been normal until she'd met up with her friend at the resort.

"So what?" Oliver muttered. "Doesn't mean shit if she decided to turn you over to the Feds. And we shouldn't even be here." Irritation laced the man's voice as he finally looked up at Brody. "There are Feds at your house in Montana and the one in Chicago. She's given them *something*. You need to be out of the country. *We* need to be out of the country."

He gritted his teeth and just nodded once because he didn't want to admit the truth out loud. No one had infiltrated his homes yet but they were being watched, and not exactly covertly. Right now, he was trying to find out if they had a warrant out for his arrest, but so far he'd gotten silence from his contacts. It was as if they were waiting on something. And the DEA agent he'd counted on for years of help wasn't answering his private phone—the number only Brody had access to. Definitely not good.

Maybe Oliver was right, and he should just leave the country. But one single private plane, only half an hour from the airport where he'd seen Layla leaving, had filed a flight plan to Redemption Harbor. She wasn't on the manifest, but...she had to have been on it.

"I'm going to kill her," he muttered, more to himself. How could Layla have betrayed him? God, he'd actually thought she might have been taken, was being held against her will. But no, she must have planned that escape with her friend. Must have been planning it before she'd even gotten to the resort. But how? He'd been watching her.

"Who?"

"Both of them," he said without thinking. He'd kill Layla and her friend. Though if it came down to having to flee or killing her, he'd save his own ass. One bitch wasn't worth him getting caught or dying. But he could lie low here for another day as Oliver searched for traces of Nova. Because that bitch would lead him to Layla. "What have you found on the friend?"

Oliver shook his head, frustrated. "Not much. A few places she frequents, but nothing solid. She rarely uses her credit card so she must use cash most of the time...which is interesting. I'm running her face through a facial recognition program and another program to pinpoint her if she shows up anywhere. I've narrowed the parameters of the search down to Redemption Harbor and the surrounding area. From what I've gathered, she is who she says she is, that much is true. But she has no social media. And she doesn't seem to have any habits or vices we can use to find her. None that I can find anyway. And her place of employment, the address…well, it doesn't exist. The building does, but it's empty. If she shows up at her house I'll know, but if Layla *is* working with the Feds, her friend won't know where she is. They'll take her to a safe house and the friend will be useless to you."

"I know." Brody just didn't care. At least killing Nova would hurt Layla. He'd kill the woman for that alone. As his rage for his fiancée—ex-fiancée—grew, he wanted to make Layla pay for what she'd done. She'd run from him. She'd left him. *Betrayed him.*

He wasn't sure what she had on him, but he didn't allow betrayal. Ever. And he was going to make her suffer as much as humanly possible. If he couldn't get his hands on her, he'd do the next best thing and kill her friend. But he wouldn't make it easy, and he wouldn't make it quick. And he'd make sure Layla found out about it.

No matter how this played out, he'd make sure Layla paid, one way or another.

CHAPTER TWENTY

—One person can change your life.—

Nova sat at the island countertop with Gage and the whole crew. Instead of meeting at the warehouse where they usually convened, they were staying low-key at Brooks's estate since Nova still had to keep her head down. At least until Kingston was caught.

Probably even after then. They weren't sure that he wouldn't come after her, but it was a risk she'd definitely been willing to take. Her best friend was worth the potential danger.

"What's wrong?" Gage murmured low enough for her ears only.

She turned slightly and gave him a half-smile, even as a low-grade ache spread across the back of her skull. "Nothing." Which was a big fat lie. A migraine was coming on, and had been for the last ten minutes. The lights in the kitchen were dim enough they weren't bothering her and it was dark out so that was a plus too. The sun could always exacerbate a migraine.

Normally she could regulate what she ate and limit her sugar intake to help, but the stress of the last week was clearly too much. And those painful little pinpricks against her skull had started. Soon she was going to excuse herself, go lie down in a dark room and put a wet cloth over her face. She desperately needed to pick up her prescription but couldn't go anywhere right now. More than anything, she simply wished she was in her own bed. Not that this estate wasn't incredible, but she simply wanted to be home.

"No lies between us." Gage's expression was intense.

Luckily no one was paying attention to them as they all talked about finding Kingston, and the Feds' current involvement with the hunt for him.

"I can feel a migraine coming on," she said, keeping her voice low. "I think the last week just proved to be too much."

His expression instantly morphed into one of concern. "What can I do?"

Okay, she really loved this man. But before she could answer, Leighton said, "Hazel's calling," even as he picked up his cell phone.

Despite the tension at the back of her head, Nova turned, completely focused on him as he took the call. There weren't many reasons why the special agent would be calling right now. She was deeply involved in the manhunt for Kingston. The warrants had come through, and the FBI and DEA had closed in on all of his homes and businesses—the two agencies were working in tandem because his crimes were apparently many. Now it was just a matter of bringing him in and seeing if they could get him to turn on the men he worked with.

"Yeah," Leighton said, all business. He nodded a few times and even though everyone was quiet, it was impossible to follow the conversation since it was mainly grunts and one-word answers on his end. "You're sure?" he asked, his tone shifting to one of excitement. Or as excited as Leighton ever got. There was a beat of silence, then, "That's great, I'll tell the others." He ended the call and turned to look at all of them.

"The Feds have Kingston cornered—he's in Redemption Harbor," he said, looking at Nova.

Surprise filtered through her at the news. There weren't many reasons he would've come to Redemption Harbor. He should have just left the country. But he must have been tracking Layla and likely had wanted to hurt Nova too.

Next to her, Gage scooted closer and wrapped an arm around her shoulders. She leaned into him as Leighton continued. The tension in her head was growing slowly but surely. But she needed to hear all of this.

"They tracked the guy he's been working with. Some low-level hacker. Nowhere near your skill, Gage."

Gage simply snorted as if that was a given. It was okay for him to be cocky. He'd earned that right.

"Can I go home?" she blurted even as she hid a wince. The ache was spreading and soon she'd be laid out on her back.

"Yeah."

"I actually think it wouldn't hurt for you to stay here a few more days," Skye interjected. "Just in case he's hired someone to come after you. You *did* help his fiancée escape. He might want payback."

"I've already put out feelers," Axel said. "There's no hit out on her or her friend Layla. And if there was, I would know about it. Not saying there won't be one in the future, but for now, she's not on any contracts. And Kingston has enough contacts that he'd hire a professional."

Nova allowed a teeny bit of relief to slide through her veins and smiled gratefully at the other man. He'd been a hit man before he'd come to work with them. "Thank you."

"We'll go to my place," Gage said, looking at her—and he wasn't asking. "No way they know where I live. Even if they've figured out that I was the man with you—and I'm ninety-nine percent sure they haven't—no one will be able to find my place. I'll keep you safe," he murmured, his voice going all sensual and heated.

Ooookay, then. He was *not* hiding anything right now. They hadn't exactly been secretive about what they'd done last night, and he'd been holding her hand this morning, but to blatantly say she'd come to his place made it pretty damn clear that they were together.

She was glad it was officially out in the open. She definitely didn't want to hide their relationship. She just nodded once at him, then turned to Leighton. "You're really sure it's okay?"

"Yep. Hazel was just giving us a heads-up. They're about to storm the place, and she said she knew she would be unavailable for the foreseeable future. They're going to be interrogating the son of a bitch as they break down his organization. She wanted to let us know you're safe."

"Good, then," Gage said abruptly as he stood. "I'm getting Nova out of here. We've had a long week and we're exhausted."

"Take as much downtime as you need," Skye said. "You guys have definitely earned it. If we need anything, we'll call."

Nova started to get up but Gage shook his head. "Sit tight. I'll go grab your stuff. Do you have any migraine medicine here?"

"No. And I'm out at my house but there's a prescription waiting at my pharmacy." She'd planned to pick it up the day after she'd gotten that text from Layla. She hadn't even thought about it until now.

"We'll pick it up on the way to my house."

"Thank you," she whispered. After everything she'd been through, she didn't want to have a breakdown over a migraine, but they were absolutely wretched. She felt weird being so vulnerable in front of Gage, but there was no one else she'd rather be with right now, even if soon she'd be holed up in his bedroom trying to block out the world. Which told her all she needed to know about her feelings for Gage. Not that she'd doubted them.

She sat back in the chair as he hurried out of the room.

Skye moved into his seat as soon as he was gone, her expression concerned. "You all right, hon? You don't look so good, and I don't mean that as an insult."

She smiled softly. She'd known the other woman for half a dozen years, and the fact that Skye had added the disclaimer that she wasn't trying to insult Nova was proof of how far Skye had come. Once upon a time, she wouldn't have bothered to add it or worry about anyone's feelings. Not because she wasn't a good person; she had the biggest heart of anyone Nova knew. But she could be very blunt and didn't always think of feelings or emotions. "I've got a migraine coming on."

"Well, Gage will take care of you. I'm glad you guys are…whatever you are."

Nova snorted softly. "We're together. He is officially my boyfriend." She liked the sound of that, even if the term boyfriend felt silly to her. And she wanted everyone to know that Gage was hers. Even Skye, her very happily married friend who viewed Gage as a brother.

"Thank God," Skye said, shaking her head. "That man has been smitten over you for too long."

Despite the tension spreading inside her, Nova smiled. She'd been smitten over him for a while too. And that wasn't changing anytime soon. Try never.

They talked for a few more minutes and, though Nova tried to keep a smile on her face, she was grateful when Gage finally returned to the kitchen, both their bags in hand.

Once they were in Gage's truck, she moved the seat back at an angle and closed her eyes, glad that Gage wasn't talking except to ask the name of her pharmacy.

Soon they'd be at his place and she could sleep. Sweet, blessed sleep.

CHAPTER TWENTY-ONE

—Fate loves the fearless.—

S weat pouring down his spine despite the cool weather, Brody sped down the two-lane highway as fast as he dared without risking drawing attention from any law enforcement. If a cop stopped him, he'd simply open fire, but that was a complication he didn't want or need right now. He was already dealing with enough shit.

He answered his phone on the first ring. "Yeah?" He'd just narrowly escaped the fucking Feds and was kicking himself for even coming to Redemption Harbor. He'd made an emotional decision, something he rarely did. It was all Layla's fault, that stupid, stupid bitch! *Everything* was her fault. He might be running now, but he swore that one day he'd find her and kill her. He'd follow the cartel's lead and burn her to death.

"Where are you?" Oliver asked. He'd left Brody a while ago to get some things before they headed out of town. If it wasn't for him, Brody never would have known the Feds were moving in on him. But Oliver had given him a heads-up that one of his own men had turned on him. Had given him up to save his own skin.

"About ten minutes to the pickup point." Instead of flying out of Redemption Harbor, he and Oliver were going to head south in a clean vehicle and fly out of a small airport in Georgia. He needed distance from here *now*. Though he wanted to make Layla suffer, she sure as hell wasn't worth getting caught. So when Oliver had found out that the Feds were swarming all over Redemption Harbor, he'd decided to cut his losses and run. *For now.*

"Look...I spotted Nova Blaire on a CCTV. Got an alert on my phone. Captured her image a few minutes ago. It's real time. I know we're leaving but thought you'd want to know."

He inwardly cursed. Oliver was basically dangling a carrot in front of him. He should just drive straight to the rendezvous point and leave, but... "Where are we on the FBI situation?"

"They're working in tandem with the DEA and about to storm the rental house they think you're inside of." Oliver had set up cameras around the location so he could watch directly from his many phones.

Brody gritted his teeth, weighing his options. "Where's the woman now?"

"According to your location, you're maybe five minutes from her." Oliver rattled off the address of a local pharmacy. He wasn't familiar with the landmarks here but he could easily look up the address.

"She alone?"

"No. She's with some guy. I didn't get a good shot of him because he's wearing a ball cap. He ducked inside the pharmacy. But there's no way to know how long he'll be. How long *they'll* even be."

"Text me the address." He didn't care. He had to go after her.

"Fuck," Oliver muttered even as Brody's burner phone pinged with an incoming text. "This is stupid."

Yeah well, then Oliver shouldn't have even told him. Brody knew why he had though. If Brody had found out later, he'd have killed Oliver for not giving him the chance to take this bitch out. "I'll be at the rendezvous point in twenty minutes." Or he hoped he would be. He had to do this. Had to hurt Layla the only way he could.

"If you're not here, I'm heading south without you. You know where the airport is. Get there if you can."

He ended the call. That would still be enough time, he realized as he looked at the clock and distance on his phone's GPS. He could be there in three minutes, smash her face in, put a bullet in her head—and the guy she was with if necessary—then be on his way. It wouldn't be as gratifying as full-on torturing her, but he wasn't bringing her along for the ride.

This had to be fate giving him a signal. She was literally right on his way to his pickup point before leaving town. Yes, she *needed* to die. Layla needed to suffer somehow. Because the bitch had betrayed him, *ruined* him. No one got away with that. If he let her turn on him with no consequences, it sent a message that he was weak. Ineffectual.

This was the universe giving him a gift. And he was going to take it.

* * *

Nova pressed her fingers to her temple, gently massaging as she remained in Gage's truck. He'd gone in to grab her prescription and though only a couple minutes had passed, it felt like an eternity. Even though she simply wanted to say screw it and head back to his place, she knew how effective the medicine was. It could cut down her agony by hours. And the last thing she wanted to do right now was be laid up at Gage's house when they could be doing much more interesting things. After the week they'd had, they deserved more of what they'd indulged in last night.

Though even that didn't sound appealing right now, for how much her head hurt.

Crash!

Her eyes snapped open as glass shattered everywhere. Two large hands shoved through the window, grabbing her by the throat and shoulder.

She clawed at Kingston's forearms as he dragged her out of the truck.

Pain splintered through her as glass slashed into her skin, but it was forgotten when he slammed her against the side of the truck.

"You stupid bitch," he snarled, pulling her back and attempting to slam her against the truck again.

Rage and adrenaline punched through her. She struck out with her free hand, slamming it into his nose, aiming for a killing blow. But the angle was wrong.

He jerked backward, his grip loosening as he grunted in pain.

She didn't waste any time. Moving swiftly, she punched him right in the throat as she lifted her good leg and nailed him in the stomach. Her punch was weak though, not as effective as it could be.

He swung blindly as he cried out, blood gushing down his face. She ducked and swiveled to the left even as she slammed out with her fist again. This time she punched him in the solar plexus.

There was no stopping her now. He'd have to kill her first. Which she knew he intended.

Too bad for him.

He flew through the air, stumbling and falling on his back. She started to run for help, because if he wasn't in that house the Feds were raiding, he might be setting them up. He was a big enough bastard to try to kill more innocent people.

She'd taken one step when Kingston swiped out at her ankle.

She fell into the side of the truck, crying out as the breath left her lungs.

220 | KATIE REUS

Adrenaline lived inside her, clawing at her, telling her to survive. And destroy him. Kicking out, she slammed her foot into his ribs. Hard.

He cried out but moved lightning fast, rolling over before she could attack again and jumping to his feet. "I should have just shot you," he snarled, reaching behind his back, no doubt for a weapon.

She didn't think, she simply reacted, her training kicking in. She rushed him, going straight for his face again as he pulled the weapon.

Everything seemed to happen in slow motion as she reared up with the heel of her palm, slamming it into his nose, driving the bone up into his skull.

She'd only ever practiced the move on dummies—obviously. The sensation now was much different, and revolting, but she felt no guilt as Kingston slumped to the cracked, gray concrete, his body sprawled over the white line demarking the next parking space.

"Nova!" Gage was suddenly in front of her, fear etched on every inch of his face as he bent down and tested Kingston's pulse.

By his relieved expression, she knew Kingston was dead. She…didn't know what to feel.

* * *

"Are you okay?" Gage asked, assessing her from head to foot as he stood, fear pulsing through him.

"Yes."

Though he wanted to take his time, make sure she was really okay, he glanced around the parking lot. He'd seen security cameras on the way in, and they were in range of what had just happened. *Hell.* A place like this wouldn't have paid guards watching the security. No, they'd just check the feeds if there was an issue.

"Should we call...Hazel? Or the cops?" Nova rasped out.

Gage made a split-second decision. "No. Get in the car."

Her eyes widened, but she did as he said. Moving quickly, Gage picked up Kingston's body and shoved the dead weight into the back seat, getting DNA and blood everywhere. He'd take care of it later. Right now, he had to do damage control and protect Nova the best way he knew how. If he broke multiple laws in the process? What else was new.

"It was self-defense," Nova said as he shut the door.

"I know," he said, sliding into the driver's seat. None of that mattered though. "How bad are you?"

"I hurt everywhere, but I'm okay." Okay was pretty relative right now, but she was alive. That was what mattered.

"I swear I'll take care of you, but I've got to dump the body. And I'm going to do something to him to make it look like he was killed by a rival cartel."

"Why? And what about security cameras?"

"I've got the cameras covered," he muttered as he pulled out of the parking spot. Thankfully it was late enough that there weren't many people here—only two other cars out front. The pharmacy itself would be closing in about twenty minutes.

He pulled around to the back of the pharmacy and didn't see any security cameras, not that it meant anything. They could be hidden. He'd be fixing that soon. He popped open the center console and pulled out a small, handheld tablet. Working quickly, he hacked into their system. Places like this didn't have people watching their feeds 24/7. Nope, the cameras were a precaution.

It took all of two minutes to erase what he needed to—and that's what they got for not changing the wireless router manufacturer's password. For good measure, he erased the entire twenty-four hours previous. It would look like a glitch, and even if it didn't, he didn't give a flying fuck. Their security was so pathetic, they deserved this.

"It's scary how well you do that," Nova murmured. "You know we might get pulled over for this window." She motioned to the broken window before she closed her eyes and leaned back against the headrest, her voice tired.

He swept his gaze over her again quickly as he pulled out of the parking lot. He gritted his teeth, hating that this had happened at all. She never should have been in a position where he hadn't been able to protect her. But he shoved all those thoughts down and compartmentalized everything. He'd berate himself later. Once she was safe. "We're not going far. I just want to dump the body somewhere close to here without cameras. Then…"

"What?"

"Shit. The Feds think he's in some house, which means he might have set them up…" He pulled out his cell phone and called Leighton.

"Yeah?" his friend answered on the first ring.

"Kingston's dead. He's in the back of my truck. Call Hazel and tell her that Kingston isn't in the house she thinks he is—don't tell her any details, just that you got a tip the man is dead. They'll find his body soon enough, trust me."

Leighton simply cursed and hung up.

"You think he set the Feds up?" Nova asked.

"It's a possibility. He's a piece of shit—or was a piece of shit. They had to get the tip somehow that he was at some random house. But it could be a tip from one of Kingston's own men."

"Why bother with all of this, making it look like someone else killed him? I didn't do anything wrong."

"I don't want him linked to you or me or our company in any way. So far we've managed to stay under the radar with all of this. Even if it was self-defense, our names will end up in a police report. We don't need any extra attention. He's dead, and that isn't changing. With his connection to the Romero cartel…no. This is the best way."

She nodded once and glanced back at Kingston's still body. "Is it weird that I don't feel guilty?"

Gage simply snorted. "No. There's no guidebook for how you're supposed to feel after something like this. And if you need counseling or whatever later, we'll make sure you get it."

"Thank you...but I don't think I will."

He drove them two miles down the road, pulled off onto the side of the two-lane highway only when there was no one else on the road, then got out and dragged Kingston's body. "Don't watch me, okay?" he asked, not wanting Nova to see what he was about to do. He wasn't sorry for it, but he didn't want her to look at him differently. He couldn't stand the thought of her being horrified by him.

"Okay." Her expression was grim as she turned in her seat.

Pulling out his knife, he moved quickly, cutting into Kingston's chest a symbol he'd seen from a file he'd hacked into. It was a brand one of the *sicarios* from the Sanchez cartel used on his victims. Since that cartel was at war with the Romeros, it was perfect. Once he was done, he grabbed a cleaning solution from the toolbox in his truck and doused the body. It should destroy any DNA.

He was back in the truck in less than sixty seconds. "Do you need to go to a hospital?" he asked. She looked rough, and even though he wanted to pull Nova into his arms and comfort her, that wasn't what she needed. She needed medical attention and they needed to get far away from Kingston's dead body.

"No. I've got some glass stuck in my arms. I need to clean up and... Oh my God, he's really dead. Can I tell Layla about this?" Her eyes were slightly dilated, and he wondered if she was going into shock.

"No. This is between you and me. I won't even tell the crew you killed him."

She blinked in surprise. "Why not?"

"Just...if anything comes back on us for this, I'm taking the heat for it."

"I won't let you do that."

He took the next turn onto a dusty road that would eventually lead to his place—a refurbished farmhouse that had once belonged to his grandparents. "Well, you won't have a choice. I'm sorry I wasn't there to protect you."

Reaching out, she gently touched his leg. "You've been a rock this last week. If it wasn't for you, I would have died in a plane crash—and even if I'd survived, I don't know that I'd have been able to get Layla away on my own. You've protected me, been my teammate, my backup...everything."

He still felt like he'd let her down somehow and it clawed at his insides. He was supposed to protect her.

She squeezed his leg. "It's okay that I protected myself too. I need to be able to look out for myself. You're not omniscient...dumbass."

Oh hell, he wouldn't laugh. He wouldn't. "Yeah...I know. It's just, if I lost you..." Hell, he couldn't even finish that thought. Not out loud and not in his head. Because he wouldn't lose her. A world without Nova? Nope.

"Are we close?" she murmured.

"Yep. Two minutes out. Just lay your head back."

"Okay." She closed her eyes, and before he'd reached his long driveway, she was breathing steadily enough that he knew she'd dozed off.

Though he hated to disturb her, he unbuckled her and helped her get out. He might not have been there to take out Kingston, but he was damn sure going to take care of her now.

Now and always.

CHAPTER TWENTY-TWO

—Be with someone who brings out the best in you.—

One week later

Nova lay stretched out on Gage's bed, content to stay exactly where she was as he finished another repetition of push-ups. The sun was barely up, but his bedroom had an entire wall of windows so she got to see *every single inch* of his half-naked body highlighted by the rising sun. All those cut lines and hard muscles were beautiful to watch.

"Seriously loving the view right now," she murmured, rolling onto her side to get a better look at him. She'd been in his house the last week as they'd waited on news from the Feds regarding the potential danger she might be in. With Kingston dead—and no one the wiser that she'd killed him—the FBI was analyzing the threat against her and any potential fallout from being involved in helping Layla run away from him.

While she felt bad about invading Gage's space so much, he didn't seem to mind. His house was huge too. Much different than what she'd expected him to live in. She'd always assumed he lived in a condo downtown, something urban and edgy. But his grandparents had left

227

him their farmhouse and he'd completely refurbished the place. It was wood, stone and glass—so much so that the place looked bigger than it was because of all the natural light. It reminded her of some of the homes she'd seen in the English countryside years ago, right down to the huge pond it overlooked. Though he'd added something to the glass so that it was impossible to see inside clearly from the outside. Now that she knew him so well, this place fit him perfectly.

Shirtless, Gage simply grinned at her as he rolled onto his back from his position on the throw rug and started doing a rep of sit-ups this time.

Yep, this was definitely the best place for her to hide out. After the insanity of killing Kingston, something she was still trying to mentally adjust to, they'd come back to his place, where she'd cleaned up—he'd helped her remove all the glass from her body and then bandaged her up—and promptly passed out in his bed. She wasn't sure if it was because of the migraine or the antibiotics he'd given her—and she still wasn't sure where he'd gotten those—but by the time she'd woken up, her migraine had been gone. She felt as if she'd been in a haze over the last week. Her life had consisted of a whole lot of sex and sleep. A lot of sleep. More than she could ever remember sleeping.

She had a feeling her brain was still trying to digest everything that had happened.

And even though she didn't feel guilty about killing Kingston, she'd had a few…not exactly nightmares, but dreams that made her feel edgy. But she was dealing with it.

When Gage's cell rang, she recognized the ring tone as Skye's—because she'd changed it to "Get The Party Started." He really shouldn't have given her his code to log in. "I'll grab it. You just keep doing what you're doing."

Laughing lightly, he continued his sit-ups.

"Hey," she said, answering the phone.

"Hey, I've got good news. You are officially out of the woods and can go home."

"Are you sure this time?" She sat up in bed, the sheet pooling around her waist.

Gage stopped what he was doing and stood, his muscular arms crossed over his chest.

"Yep. The marshals are letting Layla go now as well. There's no threat left to her, and there's definitely no threat to you. Kingston had a lot of enemies, and Layla was only a problem for him personally. Not anyone he worked with. To the cartel, you two are basically a nonissue. You especially, considering no one knows who you are anyway."

"What about the guy Kingston was working with? That hacker?"

Skye snorted. "That jackass was killed three days ago in a holding cell."

"Seriously? By who?" The Feds had ended up finding the guy trying to escape town. After one of Kingston's men had told the Feds where to find Kingston, and how he and the hacker would be escaping town, it had only been a matter of time before they'd be caught anyway. The combined forces of the FBI and the DEA had spread their net wide and ended up catching Kingston's hacker buddy. They would have got Kingston too—if he hadn't been dead already.

"Someone linked to the Romero cartel."

Nova frowned. "But that's the one Kingston worked with."

"Yep. Looks like they didn't want to risk that his buddy talked to anyone."

"Are there any questions about Kingston's death?" So far there hadn't been, but Nova couldn't help the kernel of worry that still lived inside her.

"Nope. They're chalking it up to cartel violence. No one cares who killed him. Least of all the DEA. They're glad he's gone, considering he killed one of their own."

"What about the dirty agent?"

"Not our problem. He won't be getting out of jail anytime soon. If ever. And he's definitely not a problem for Layla or you. Some of Kingston's guys are willing to testify against him for a reduced sentence—and they've got more stuff on him than the shit with Kingston. You guys mean nothing to him."

She had more questions but the only thing she really cared about now was her best friend. "So what about Layla?"

"Well, I was hoping to surprise you, but I'm not going to lie. I'm on my way to pick her up now. I can meet you at Gage's or at your house. Whichever one you want."

"My place. I'll head out of here as soon as we get off the phone. Thank you so much for getting her," Nova said, elation filling her. Layla must be thrilled right now, and she couldn't wait to hug her best friend.

"No worries. I'll text you when we're en route."

Once they disconnected, she dropped Gage's phone onto the comforter next to her and smiled at him as he scooted closer. "I'm okay to go home. And so is Layla. Skye is on her way to get her. She's going to bring her to my place. There's no threat to either of us anymore."

He let out a relieved breath and leaned forward to brush his lips over hers. "Good," he murmured.

She knew that Gage had been monitoring the whole situation, and she'd been fairly certain that soon enough she'd be able to go home, but it had happened quicker than she'd planned. Part of her was sad to be leaving Gage's place, but it wasn't as if she could simply move in here. It was way too soon, and of course he would want his space. But she was going to miss waking up to his sexy face every morning.

"Let me grab a quick shower and change and we'll head out," he said before dropping another kiss on her lips.

"Sounds good." She needed to get dressed too. When she heard the shower start running, she grabbed all of her things and packed her bags. A bittersweet sensation settled inside her—she was ecstatic to see Layla, and to know that the threat had lifted, but she was really going to miss being at Gage's house.

It was a good thing though. Now everyone could all return to their normal lives. Though she wondered what normal would look like for her and Gage. Now that everything had died down, she also wondered what her place in his life would look like. Because she was serious about him and wanted everything from him. She knew he was serious about her too, but they hadn't talked much about the future.

She was certain she wanted a future with him though.

* * *

Nova stepped into her kitchen to find Gage working away on his laptop. Earlier, he'd mentioned something about a potential new job for the crew, so she guessed it was related to that. "Layla just headed upstairs. She said she's exhausted. Not that I blame her."

Her friend was handling things exceptionally well, considering all that she'd been through. For the last week, she'd been in a state of limbo, not knowing if she'd be able to return to her life. Then suddenly today, she'd been released into the real world.

"You didn't have to hide out in here the whole time," she murmured. Skye had met Gage and Nova at her house with Layla in tow a couple hours ago, and Gage had mostly hung out in the kitchen, leaving the two of them to talk in the living room.

"I know. But she's your best friend and I didn't want you to feel crowded."

The man was so damn considerate. She walked around the center island and reached for him, glad when he immediately stepped into her embrace and hugged her tight. She buried her face against his chest and inhaled. He was such a steady presence in her life—and the sexiest man on the planet.

She wanted to tell him she loved him but every time she tried to get the words out, her throat froze up. Which was stupid, considering everything they'd been through. But she'd never told a man that she loved him before, and she could admit she had issues where family and relationships were concerned. What if it was too soon and Gage thought she was nuts for telling him?

"What's she planning to do now? Move back to Montana?" he asked quietly, rubbing a hand up and down her back, all sweet and sensual.

"For now at least, she's going to stay with me. She'll go home to get all her stuff, but she doesn't want to move back there." Nova stepped back slightly but still kept her arms around him as she looked up at him. "I've got the room, so there's no reason she can't move in. She plans to go back to teaching. It won't take much for her to earn the required accreditation for South Carolina. Then she'll start putting out her resume. Considering her degrees and how good she is with kids, it won't take long for her to find a job."

Gage was silent for a long moment. "You're okay with having a roommate?"

Nova snorted softly. "We've lived together before. Layla is the neatest, most considerate roommate I could ever ask for. And she cooks. Trust me, in this equation, I'm the 'bad' roommate. It will be a little weird living with someone again, but she needs a new place to start over. And I'll admit I'm selfish—I miss having my best friend around."

He cleared his throat. "Just a thought, but if you wanted to let her just live here...you could move in with me." His tone was neutral, surprising her. He just said the words as if he hadn't dropped a giant bomb on her.

"Wait...what? Are you asking me to move in with you?"

"Maybe."

"There is no maybe in this, dumbass. You're either asking me or you're not."

He grinned, all sexy and mischievous. "God, I love your pet names."

She pinched his side. "Well?"

"It depends on what your answer is."

She narrowed her gaze slightly at him. "I've never lived with a man before."

"There's a first time for everything. And for the record, I've never lived with a woman before either. Look, I love you, Nova—"

"I love you too!" she blurted, interrupting his own declaration.

At her words, his grin spread to epic proportions. "All right, then. We love each other. We've literally been in a plane crash together. I want to live with you. I want to wake up and see your face every morning—I want to bury my face between your legs more mornings than not. I'm not going anywhere, Nova. You're it for me. I won't use the M-word—yet—but you should know that a proposal is coming soon. You. Are. Mine."

"Gage..." She sucked in a sharp breath at his words. *What. The. Heck.* M-word, as in marriage? For some reason...the thought didn't terrify her.

Okay, not for some reason. Because of Gage. The man owned her.

"You don't have to say anything. I'm just putting my cards on the table."

"Okay, then." She paused for a long moment, looking into his bluish-gray eyes. "I need to talk to Layla first, to see how she'll feel about living here by herself, but yes, I want to move in with you." Like yesterday.

Grinning like he'd just hacked the Pentagon, Gage leaned down and brushed his lips over hers, but soon that chaste kiss turned into something deeper, more heated. Then she found herself hoisted up onto the island countertop as he threaded his fingers through her hair, holding her tight. Heat flooded her body, warmth pooling between her legs as she imagined him taking her right here on the counter. She could turn around, bend over the countertop…but… She pressed a gentle hand against his chest.

Breathing hard, he pulled back a fraction. "What?"

"We can't do this in here," she whispered. "Let's head up to my room." She could be quiet. She hoped. She'd try anyway.

He nodded and, surprising her, scooped her up and headed for the stairs. All the muscles in her body tightened at the hungry look in his gaze. Oh yeah, she'd have to work at being quiet this time.

CHAPTER TWENTY-THREE

—Never apologize for doing the right thing.—

"Why are we all here?" Gage practically snarled as he sat at the conference table. Skye had called all of them to this meeting but hadn't said much other than they all needed to talk. Nova hadn't moved into Gage's place yet—they needed to pack all her things—but she had stayed over at his place last night. And Skye had interrupted them. Which was a cardinal fucking sin as far as he was concerned.

"Babe," Nova murmured as she squeezed his hand. "Chill."

Okay, he *was* kind of cranky. Now that he had Nova in his life—and in his bed—interruptions this early in the morning were *not* welcome.

"The meeting was actually my idea," Leighton said as he stepped into the room, Hazel with him.

Gage straightened slightly, surprised to see the special agent there. The warehouse-turned-office space was sacred to all of them. Outsiders were not welcome. And no matter how much Hazel had helped them, she was an outsider.

"Thank you all for meeting me here," Hazel said, looking at each of them. "What I'm going to tell you

237

could get me fired, which is why I'm not leaving an electronic trail for this. We know who targeted your plane," she said, looking at Brooks. "It has nothing to do with you or Redemption Harbor Consulting. Your father was the target—the man who wanted to kill him thought the plane was his, not yours. A right-wing nut who hates—hated—your father, specifically because of some business deals he made, targeted him. But at the end of the day, he was targeted because he's wealthy. The method the man used to cause the failure on the plane is one we've seen before—twice. We were able to track the guy down. He was killed when he shot at our agents."

"What about the pilot though?" Gage asked.

"He added a sedative to the entire supply of water bottles at the hangar—in the pilots' office—so it targeted any of the pilots you guys happened to use. Dwayne Wilson—that's the guy—was playing the odds by sabotaging the plane and attempting to knock out the pilot."

"The pilot was dead, not just knocked out." Gage was certain of that.

Her expression was grim. "According to the coroner, the pilot had a heart condition." She pulled out a file and set it in front of Gage. "You can read the details about why he died. The sedative mixed with his heart meds caused it. Once you're satisfied, I need the files back. I can't leave this with you guys."

Gage flipped it open and quickly scanned the information, including filing away the name of the man who'd almost gotten him and Nova killed. "You sure this guy's dead?" He was going to check up and see if the man had any partners. If so, they were dead men walking.

Her grin was just a little bit feral. "Yes. I wasn't there, obviously, because I've been busy in Redemption Harbor. But that hillbilly is dead. And we don't think he was working with anyone else. Douglas isn't the only billionaire he'd targeted. The guy was smart. Just not smart enough."

Gage wanted more details about who else the man had targeted but he could discover that on his own.

"How long are you in Redemption Harbor?" Leighton asked.

She lifted a shoulder. "As long as it takes to wrap all this up. We're working with the DEA right now, and at this point we're basically just filling out paperwork. I'll probably head back to DC in a couple days."

All right, then. That was that. Gage considered this chapter closed. Kingston was dead and so was the man who'd almost gotten the woman he loved killed.

As soon as Hazel was gone, Skye stood from her chair then leaned against the table before she started pacing. She never could stay still. She was like a ping-pong ball, always moving. "I feel like we got lucky with this—and lucky is probably the wrong word. But it could've been Kuznetsov who came after us. This just as easily could have been a targeted attack."

Brooks softly snorted. "If it had been Kuznetsov, he would have targeted us simultaneously."

They all nodded even as Skye said, "Exactly. We're not sitting ducks, but sometimes it feels like it. We need to take Kuznetsov down and end the threat of him once and for all."

"He has a lot of businesses. We can target him through one of those. Make it appear as if one of his own people killed him," Gage said. "Because it can't look like *any* of us are linked to his death. Unlike this last job, cutting off the head will simply piss off the people beneath him. Or at least we're taking a bigger risk of that happening." Kuznetsov was more or less organized crime, which meant his people were loyal to him. So they had to make it look as if he was killed by a rival or someone in his own organization. It was the only way to keep all of them safe and free from retribution.

"You're likely not a threat to him anymore," Skye said, focusing on Brooks, her reference to the "peace treaty" the two men had come to nearly a year ago clear. "This is the perfect time to start doing recon on him. Well, more than we already have."

"I'm in," Savage said quietly.

Everyone else nodded their agreement, including Gage and Nova.

"We'll have to tell Mercer and Mary Grace," Nova said quietly. "They might not work with us, but they're still our family."

"Agreed." Skye nodded once.

Gage was glad they were going after Kuznetsov. The man needed to be brought down, and sooner rather than later. He was a monster, and whether or not they had a peace treaty of sorts with the guy, shit like that never lasted long. Sooner or later, Kuznetsov would come after Brooks because Brooks had subtly threatened a daughter Kuznetsov kept secret from the world, in order to protect Darcy, the woman he loved. It was very likely that Kuznetsov would one day go scorched earth and kill everyone close to Brooks, because that was exactly how the mobster operated.

For the moment, however, Gage shelved thoughts of the gangster and tugged Nova onto his lap.

She let out a yelp of surprise but willingly moved, ignoring a few of the snickers from the others. He leaned close and brushed his mouth against her ear. "As soon as we're done here, we're going to be back at my place and I'm going to be deep inside you, making you scream my name."

Her cheeks flushed, just as he'd hoped, but she didn't respond. She simply wiggled once over his lap, torturing him. He bit back a groan. The woman knew exactly what she was doing.

He wasn't sure how he'd lived without her before. His world had been gray until she'd walked into it, and he hadn't even realized it. He was definitely a lucky man. Which was another reason Kuznetsov needed to die. There was no way they could simply make sure he went to jail.

No, he needed to be eliminated completely. The man ran drugs, but more importantly, he trafficked people.

That was the kind of shit Gage wouldn't put up with. Ever. The mobster needed to be stopped for that alone. And for the threat he posed to all of them.

CHAPTER TWENTY-FOUR

—Strive for progress not perfection.—

One month later

Nova stepped onto the patio of the Italian restaurant that Douglas Alexander had rented out for Axel and Hadley's rehearsal dinner. He'd pulled out all the stops for his daughter's wedding, even if it was a fairly small one. Just renting out a room wasn't good enough—he wanted the whole place available for his little girl. Hard not to adore the older man for that. He treated her like a princess.

They'd just come from the actual rehearsal and Nova was looking forward to dinner, which was supposed to be incredible here. Right now, everyone was mingling and getting drinks, and since she'd already had two glasses of champagne, she needed food pretty soon.

"What's up, guys?" she asked as she looked between Olivia, Skye, and Valencia.

Olivia looked furious, something that Nova had never seen before. Well, maybe not furious, but she looked seriously annoyed. *With Skye.* Petite and fragile looking—though Nova knew the woman wasn't fragile—Olivia had her hands on her hips as she glared at Skye.

Which was just taking her life into her own hands, as far as Nova was concerned. Skye was terrifying—she literally carried explosives in her purse—"For good measure."

"Skye apparently decided to teach my daughter to pick pockets," Olivia snapped, her gaze not leaving Skye's.

"Oh, I thought you knew about that by now," Nova blurted before she could rein in her big fat mouth. Yep, she definitely did not need a third glass of champagne at the rate she was going.

Olivia swiveled, her dark eyes going wide. "You knew about this?"

"Yes. No. I don't know. I think I've had too much to drink. I don't even know what I'm saying at this point." She took a step back toward the French doors she'd come through. *Escape, escape!*

"You're such a liar. Who else knew about this?"

"Nobody?" *Gah.* Her lying skills were beyond subpar.

Valencia, who'd recently turned seven, giggled, but slapped a hand over her mouth when Olivia turned back to frown at her. Oh no. This was a mess she'd never get out of.

With Olivia's back turned, Nova took the opportunity to escape and hurried back through the door and shut it behind her. When she saw Colt, she shook her head. "I would not go out there. Olivia just found out about Skye's extracurricular activities with Valencia."

Colt just snorted and headed outside anyway. Nova figured that if he was married to Skye, Olivia's fury wouldn't faze him at all.

Smiling when she saw Layla at a high-top table in the little bar/bistro area, talking to Gage, she headed over there. Since moving in with him, she'd thought there might be a weird transition period, but he'd given her more than half his closet and seemed to relish all the space she was taking up. It felt almost too good to be true.

"What's going on outside?" Layla whispered even though there were only a few other people in the bar area and no one was paying attention to them.

"Skye's in trouble with Olivia."

Gage laughed, the sound wrapping around her, warming her inside and out. "I can't believe it's taken her this long to figure it out. Valencia went around pickpocketing everybody during the rehearsal. Olivia found all the knickknacks in her flower girl basket."

"Holy crap, and you're just now telling me this?" Nova vaguely wondered if Valencia had taken anything from her.

"I just found out about it from Savage. I think she snagged your eyeliner."

Nova laughed at the ridiculousness of it all. "Where is he anyway?"

"Pretty sure he's hiding somewhere so he doesn't have to be involved with punishing Valencia. He's such a softy where she's concerned."

"I can't blame the guy," Nova said. "She's adorable."

Layla looked between the two of them. "I can't believe this. Skye was seriously teaching a little girl how to steal?"

"Oh yeah. It's been going on for a while. She's taught her how to pick locks as well. And I'm pretty sure next up is breaking into safes. But in Skye's defense... Yeah, I don't know what I can say to defend her." Nova snort-giggled at that. The whole thing really was ridiculous but it was a miracle that Olivia hadn't known about it.

Layla giggled lightly. "Oh my gosh, you do not need any more champagne."

"I *know*. At least not until I have some food in my stomach. So...who was that man you were talking to at the rehearsal earlier?" Nova had been dying to find out about the giant Layla had been semi-flirting with. The man looked kinda scary, and the only thing Nova knew was that he was somehow friends with Axel. And it was hard not to wonder if the guy was in the profession Axel used to be in.

Layla's cheeks flushed slightly and she shrugged. "Just some man."

Nova's gaze narrowed. "You know I can just sic Gage on the guy and he'll dig up every single thing about his past if you don't tell me who he is."

"No way." Gage stood and dropped a kiss on her cheek. "I'm staying out of this. You're not using me as your hired hacker."

Layla snickered as Gage hurried away from their table. "You really landed a good one with him. He looks at you as if you hung the damn moon."

"Yeah, I really did. He's amazing." And sexy—and a god in bed. But she kept all that to herself. "I'm so glad you guys get along so well too."

"It's kind of hard not to like the guy who helped save my life." At that, Layla's expression shuttered just a bit, but enough for Nova to notice.

"You doing okay with everything?" It had been over a month since she'd settled in Redemption Harbor, and she seemed to be doing well. She was substitute teaching until she found something permanent, and Nova saw her a few times a week.

"I'm fine. Sometimes it just hits me that I almost married a monster. I still can't believe I didn't see *through* him. It makes me question everything."

"You're not omniscient. You did nothing wrong. You fell for someone who treated you right—for the most part. He put on a mask for you and the rest of the world."

"I know that. I really do. At least in my head. Trying to convince the rest of me that it's true and just accept the fact is what I keep getting hung up on. But enough about that. Tonight is supposed to be fun."

"You planning to have fun with your mystery man later?"

"Uh, no. I don't even trust my taste in men anymore. But he was fun to flirt with."

Nova thought the man looked kind of terrifying, with his scarred face and his huge size alone, but she wasn't going to judge. She simply shrugged. "What's this I heard about you taking Skye to a spa day? Was that a joke?"

Layla laughed. "Oh, it's not a joke. I convinced her to get a salt scrub body treatment and a pedicure—a stone massage one. Though to be fair, I appealed to her pragmatic side. She runs a lot and needed the massage. But she drew the line at a manicure. Still, I even convinced her to do one of those pottery classes with me next week—if she's in town. She's so much fun."

"I...can't believe it." Nova had known Skye a long time too. But around Layla, Skye was a different version of herself. A slightly softer one.

"Well, she only agreed to the pottery class if I agreed to go to the shooting range with her. Apparently she's going to give me shooting lessons." Layla rolled her eyes.

Nova simply shook her head. For as long as she'd known Layla, her best friend had always taken in strays of sorts. She seemed to attract a certain type of person to her, and she looked out for them. That's actually why Nova thought she'd fallen for Kingston in the first place. Not because he was that type of person, but because he'd taken care of Layla and she'd simply allowed it to happen. For once, her friend hadn't been the one taking care of someone. But all of that had been an illusion.

Regardless, Nova loved that Layla and Skye had become so close as well. Skye might think that she'd taken Layla under her wing, but Nova was pretty certain it was the other way around. Layla had a way of bringing out the best in people.

—You can't be sad when you're holding a cupcake.—

Nova kicked her legs out on the chaise lounge on Gage's back deck. Well, technically it was hers too, she guessed. He kept reminding her that it was *their* place now, not just his. But it felt weird to say it or even think it.

Despite the chilly weather, it was perfect outside. With the stone fire pit going and her very sexy boyfriend sitting down with a tray of two glasses of champagne—and cupcakes!—life was pretty damn good.

"You're officially my hero now." She debated between the cupcake and champagne and snagged the glass first. They'd just finished a pretty intense job and now were gearing up for something even bigger, something that would require the whole team's effort. She could definitely go for some bubbly right about now.

He kissed her once before sitting down next to her and stretching his own legs out. "Hey, will you call Skye for me? I need to ask her something and I left my phone inside."

She snorted. "So lazy," she said, giggling even as she picked up her cell phone.

Almost immediately, she frowned. A bunch of foreign symbols were scattered across the screen. Oh hell, her phone better not have a virus.

"You might have to get your phone after all," she muttered. But her frown deepened as the symbols fit together like a puzzle piece to form...a diamond ring?

Then the words *MARRY ME?* flashed across her phone—and when she turned to look at Gage, she found him on one knee next to the chair, an open ring box in hand.

She blinked at the phone and then at him. Sneaky, wonderful man! "Yes!"

He grinned and pulled the ring out of the box. As he slid it on her finger, he said, "Yes, you *will* marry me?"

"*Yes*, I'll marry you. Whenever you want, wherever you want." Sooner rather than later, she thought. Tomorrow if he wanted. The man owned her heart.

"Thank God." He pulled her into his arms as he stood, and a second later her favorite song came through the speakers hidden on his back deck. *Very* sneaky man.

He guided her away from the chairs and closer to the fire pit. "I can't wait to make you my wife," he murmured, looking at her with the most intense, sweetest expression she'd ever seen.

"And I can't wait to *be* your wife... I guess that'll make me Mrs. Dumbass when you're being one, huh?"

Gage threw back his head and laughed, the pure joy in his expression something she would remember forever.

Thank you for reading HUNTING DANGER, the latest book in the Redemption Harbor series. If you don't want to miss any future releases, please feel free to join my newsletter. Find the signup link on my website:

https://www.katiereus.com

ACKNOWLEDGMENTS

It's that time again where I thank all the people who help make my books better. First, Kari, thank you a billion times over for reading this book and every other book and offering your valuable insight. All my books are stronger because of you, especially this one. For Sarah, thank you for all your be-hind-the-scenes work. You are a life saver. I'm also grateful to Kelli and Julia for their editing expertise! For Jaycee, yet another cover I'm in love with. Thank you. For my wonder-ful readers, it's because of you that this series is going strong. As always, I'm thankful to my husband for not only his sup-port, but also answering technical questions I get hung up on. Thank you for helping me with the little details. Last but not least, I'm thankful to God for everything.

COMPLETE BOOKLIST

Red Stone Security Series
No One to Trust
Danger Next Door
Fatal Deception
Miami, Mistletoe & Murder
His to Protect
Breaking Her Rules
Protecting His Witness
Sinful Seduction
Under His Protection
Deadly Fallout
Sworn to Protect
Secret Obsession
Love Thy Enemy
Dangerous Protector
Lethal Game

Redemption Harbor Series
Resurrection
Savage Rising
Dangerous Witness
Innocent Target
Hunting Danger
Covert Games

The Serafina: Sin City Series
First Surrender
Sensual Surrender
Sweetest Surrender
Dangerous Surrender

ABOUT THE AUTHOR

Katie Reus is the *New York Times* and *USA Today* bestselling author of the Red Stone Security series, the Darkness series and the Deadly Ops series. She fell in love with romance at a young age thanks to books she pilfered from her mom's stash. Years later she loves reading romance almost as much as she loves writing it.

However, she didn't always know she wanted to be a writer. After changing majors many times, she finally graduated summa cum laude with a degree in psychology. Not long after that she discovered a new love. Writing. She now spends her days writing dark paranormal romance and sexy romantic suspense.

For more information on Katie please visit her website: www.katiereus.com. Also find her on twitter @katiereus or visit her on facebook at:
www.facebook.com/katiereusauthor.

Made in the USA
Coppell, TX
15 March 2020

16852640R00152